MISTY

LYREBIRD LAKE BOOK 2

FIONA MCARTHUR

ABOUT THE AUTHOR

Fiona McArthur has written more than forty-five books and shares her medical knowledge and her love of working with women, families and emergency services in her stories.

In her compassionate, pacy fiction, her love of the travel and the Australian landscape meshes beautifully with warm, funny, multigenerational characters as she highlights challenges for rural and remote families, overseas adventures, and the strength shared between women.

There will be romance. Fiona means to make that gorgeous heroic man earn the right to win his beautiful and strong-willed heroine's heart because absolutely, happy endings are a must.

Fiona is the author of the non-fiction book *Aussie Midwives,* and lives on a farm with her husband in northern New South Wales. She was awarded the NSW Excellence in Midwifery Award in 2015. The NZ Koru Award in 2019 for short romantic fiction and the Australian RUBY Award for Contemporary Romantic Fiction 2020. Find her at FionaMcArthurAuthor.com

To midwives, mothers, and writing friends. You have made my life rich in magic moments.

Special mention to dear buddies Bronwyn Jameson and Trish Morey who are there for me in my hours (lots of them) in need. Thank you to Raelene Dal Santo and Roby Aiken for their casting eyes. And to my darling husband, Ian, you make me smile.

And, always to you, dear Reader, my gratitude.

MISTY

CHAPTER 1

Misty

Through sparkling lights she saw seagulls. And a circle of shells.

Misty Buchanan knew it was the start of a premonition because she'd come to recognise them over the years.

Argh. Not today, not while fishing on this deserted beach with South West Rocks Lighthouse in the distance and the wind in her hair. Her last day at the beach before she moved to inland Queensland. She'd been so caught up in the pleasure of the salty breeze, the turquoise waves full of fish that teased and fascinated her in every curling water wall, she didn't want to be pulled away.

Her sight shimmered and dimmed and she accepted she had no choice but to watch as she closed her eyes.

When younger, it had frightened Misty to see people

and situations with such clarity while her eyes were shut but now she accepted it as part of her life, albeit a small part, for only rarely did the future affect her present so vividly.

With this gift came responsibility and her heart thumped with the double-edged sword of what could be revealed and what might be expected of her.

The man balanced on a jumbled spit of rocks beside flapping seagulls, and in the haze of the future his torso looked tough and lean against the backdrop of the ocean. He cradled one bird against him gently to unwind the twine. She couldn't see his face but there was something about his concern for the tangled gull that felt familiar on a different level.

The seagull in his hand pulled free with the last of the twine and he stepped back out of the way. His foot slipped, he teetered...

Misty leaned forward, squeezing her eyes tighter, and the mists cleared again. She drew her breath in sharply as the movie continued.

His head smashed against the rocks as he fell and then his body rolled into a green wave and the long torso and limbs began to wash without direction away from the rocks.

The vision dissipated and she knew she'd been shown all she would be. If she could get there before he fell, maybe she could stop him.

Misty's fingers clenched on her beach rod as she reeled in as fast as she could, then spun to swoop up her empty bucket so she could race towards her Jeep. Once there she tossed them into the back haphazardly as her gaze scanned the distance for clues.

The beach stretched for miles both ways and each

ended with a rocky outcrop into the ocean. In the distance a flock of gulls soared below the tall white lighthouse over a rock-tumbled outcrop.

Visions never came without the opportunity to somehow influence the course of events. She'd have to trust to instinct as she slewed the vehicle with reckless speed through the sand towards the lighthouse.

FIVE MINUTES later Misty's vehicle slid to a halt and she grabbed the board she kept for body surfing and dragged it behind her. The hot sand squeaked beneath her feet in protest as she tore across the beach. She had to leap to reach the grainy boulders of the outcrop and the rough rocks scratched skin from her soles. That would sting tomorrow.

All she could do was pray this was the correct headland. It was possible. There were birds circling, gulls as she'd seen behind closed eyes.

She stared, straining to see into the choppy green water between the swells for any sign of a body. Her stomach plummeted. Nothing. If he was already in there, he was drowning.

Was it the wrong headland?

As she turned to race back to the car her final glance caught the roll of a long brown arm and then she saw the rest of his limp body as he slid face down along the back of a wave.

'Help,' she muttered unhappily as she looked at the rocks that broke the swells as they drove into the headland. 'Come on, Misty. Big breath,' she encouraged herself as she scrambled inelegantly to the water's edge and dived into the next wave with the board beneath her. Her breath sucked in as the cold water splashed around her and dormant resuscitation drills, reinforced yearly at the hospital and the surf lifesaving club at Coffs Harbour, pounded into her mind as she paddled furiously towards her target.

The occasional swell washed over her face and she spat out salty water as she tried to calculate how long he could have been unconscious.

That first touch when she grasped his arm gave her a rush of relief; his skin was still warm even in the water. She heaved him towards her and flung his arm over the edge of the board, slipping off herself to tread water beside him.

By default his head rose from the water as the next wave lifted him half over the board and water ran from his mouth. She sank below the surface to push his other shoulder onto the boogie board. When his weight came off her, she could rest.

'Hello,' she shouted. 'Wake up. Open your eyes.'

No response when she shook his arm.

Twice, awkwardly, she blew into his cold lips, but it was hard to keep their lips locked together in the rocking water. Twice he didn't respond.

Another wave washed over them. She needed to get him to shore.

'Stay with me,' she urged into his ear as she dragged the board around to face the beach. The desperate urgency of his condition propelled her through the water, legs pumping hard and fast, her breath gasping to fill her own lungs with the effort.

Three more puffs into his mouth between swells and then a larger swell closed in on them and she angled the board so that they were lifted swiftly towards the beach.

Another big swell carried them until a sudden green monster wave swept them forward and tumbled them in an ungainly pile of limbs and board in the shallows. It felt like forever but had been bare minutes.

She spat out seawater as she twisted on her side to hang onto him.

The wave that had been powerful enough to throw them onto the sand now seemed intent on pulling them back. He began to slip and she knew she didn't have the strength to return to the water after him.

'Come on,' she gritted between her teeth and with a desperate heave she yanked him from the ocean's tenacious grip. The wave receded and it was then she noticed the tiny rivulets of his blood that went with it.

Misty dragged in welcome air before she rolled him over and pulled him an extra foot away from the reach of the next wave. His eyes were open, blue like his lips, and his white face was as unmoving as his chest as the water drained away from around him.

Cold fear slammed into her. It was too late!

She bent to lay her ear against his battered chest. Thump... Thump... Thump... She could hear it. He had a heartbeat.

It was slow, less than forty beats a minute she estimated, but so much better than no heartbeat at all. So, breathing was the problem.

She pushed him onto his side and water trickled from his mouth, but still he didn't move.

She shook him and he rolled onto his back. 'Hey. Wake up, big guy!'

Misty tilted his head and after a quick glance to check his airway was clear she breathed two quick breaths into his lungs as she watched his chest rise. Yes! Out of the water now she could tell there was chest movement.

She pushed rhythmically on the lower third of his sternum to compress his ribcage and prayed cardiac massage would speed his sluggish heart. Thirty quick depressions, then Misty pinched his nose and blew into his mouth again.

After several desperate cycles he twitched and finally stirred, his chest moved of its own volition, and he gurgled a bubbling stream of sea water as he instinctively rolled his face to the side.

A single sob slipped from Misty and she sat back on her heels, dragged her hand across her mouth and drew deep panting breaths of her own as the stranger coughed and wheezed his way to life.

Her shoulders began to shake in earnest as shock seeped through her body and she wrapped her arms around her chest in comfort as she stared down at him. Hot tears trickled unchecked down her cheeks along with a strangled gasp of mixed euphoria and horror. She sucked another big breath to calm herself and squeezed her arms around her body harder.

Focus.

Don't fall to pieces yet.

She could hardly believe it. He was alive.

She glanced out at the ocean in incredulity and saw her pretty pink boogie board bobbing merrily in the swells as it drifted out to sea.

She glanced down at the broken strap on her wrist and strained to remember when it had sheared.

Who cared? Someone would enjoy the board when it found land.

CHAPTER 2

Ben

*B*en Moore hovered in a beam of light and stared down at his body as it floated in the water. He dreamed in waves that defined his life. Each swell contained an ocean of memories.

His daughter's birth.

His wife's death.

A patient's family hugging him after a baby's first breath.

A mermaid with long auburn hair and green eyes holding out her hand.

His daughter had loved mermaids. He smiled at the irony. He was definitely dying.

Something jolted him and he felt himself fall.

The other pictures faded until only her vivid emerald eyes remained and those eyes came closer as she kissed him.

Then he was coughing and retching and reality crashed in on him along with the fire in his lungs and the pain in his pounding head.

When the fire settled he took another tearing breath and hoped to avoid the painful mix of seawater and air but it was not to be.

When that convulsion died down he eased his shoulders from the gritty sand on which he was lying and ran his hands over his lacerated chest.

The surging waves lapped his feet and above him knelt the mermaid in person — except she had long gorgeous legs in tattered denim shorts. Definitely not a mermaid then, he thought fuzzily. He noted her fine-boned arms and the slender frame that was clearly outlined in the singlet top plastered to her skin.

How on earth had she dragged him in?

As if she knew what he was thinking her voice washed over him, warm and reassuring, and the fact that he could hear the sound as her beautiful mouth moved meant he really had survived.

'We rode a wave to shore. I pulled you the rest of the way,' she said. 'Apart from almost drowning, you've hit your head and torn your skin on the rocks.'

Her long red hair was tied in a limp ponytail that dripped silver rivulets of seawater between her breasts and she flipped it over to her back, which helped the thin singlet plaster itself even closer to her breasts. He sucked his breath in with disastrous results and when that spasm passed, the air in his lungs finally began to feel less like lava and more like the cooler gravel he needed to survive.

'Thank you.' Finally, cracked words emerged. He

inhaled gingerly again. 'What happened?' Amazing how much energy those few words took.

'Don't talk yet.' She winced at his obvious discomfort and her hand slid down over his wrist, smooth and cool and very practised as she palpated his pulse.

She looked satisfied with what she felt. 'I guess you fell into the water and hit your head. You nearly drowned.'

She was looking at him as if he might not understand but he understood all right. He'd slipped. Hit his head. And should have drowned. She'd saved his life and put her own very much at risk to do so. He just couldn't think of anything to say at the moment.

'I need to get you to a hospital for observation,' she continued. He closed his eyes as he listened to her talk more to herself than to him. 'Saltwater can cause delayed pulmonary oedema in your lungs.'

He dragged himself into a sitting position and that hurt less than lying down trying to breathe. Ben rocked his head gently and couldn't help the groan that escaped as the pain from his skull intensified. It hurt like hell but he didn't want a hospital. He wanted his bed. To be alone.

'Thank you.' He paused for breath. 'Just my shack.' He paused again. 'I'll be fine.'

He watched her roll her eyes and it amused him in a ridiculous, semi-hysterical way. No doubt it was the euphoria of having been snatched from the jaws of death.

She stood. 'You need a proper check-up. Does your head swim?'

He put his hand up for her to grasp. 'Better than my body does when I'm knocked out.'

'A joker,' she muttered. 'Just what I need.'

Mermaid took his hand and shared his weight as he

rose, but he swayed against her before he could steady himself and they both knew he was hanging on to his balance by sheer willpower.

The feel of her soft hand was his only warmth and he looked down at her fingers as they curled around his own. He frowned at the strangeness of a connection that shouldn't even have registered, not understanding it, then shrugged the thought away. At this moment he needed all his strength to stagger to her vehicle.

That was enough to contend with.

CHAPTER 3

Misty

$\mathcal{M}$isty opened the door and the stranger slumped into her passenger seat. His head lolled against the headrest as if he could barely support its weight.

'You okay?' She reached across hard abs and a wide chest to buckle his seat belt.

He mumbled something she didn't catch and Misty stared anxiously into his shadowed face as she leaned back into her own seat. She studied him.

The strong line of his jaw and angled cheeks were softened by spiky bristle, as if he hadn't shaved that day. Funny how that darkened stubble in no way detracted from his rugged good looks. The longer she looked the more attractive he seemed.

More attractive? Ouch! Mind on job, she admonished herself silently. First, he had to recover.

'Hello, Big Guy? Wake up.' She rested her hand on his damp shoulder. 'I need directions if you want me to take you home.'

She was definitely having second thoughts about leaving him alone in some beach shack to die. If he started to look worse than he did now, she'd ring her brother. Even though Andy's hospital at Lyrebird Lake was hours away, his advice would help.

'I'm awake.' He didn't open his eyes, but his words emerged clearly this time, recuperative devil, and she felt the tension ease a fraction from her neck. He paused, as if it hurt to talk, and she realised it probably did. Der.

'Name's Ben Moore,' he said. 'My beach shack's about two kilometres along out of the national park.' He paused again. 'There's a side road past the camping ground on the left.' Without opening his eyes, he added, 'You can drive around the gate instead of opening it. You'll see the sign. Benmore.'

'Like the gardens in Scotland or like your name?' she asked as she steered the vehicle across the sand. He didn't answer and that was okay with Misty. She had enough to concentrate on, navigating the thick sand of the track while her Jeep slewed sideways over the mounds made by other off-road vehicles.

Once she hit the hard dirt the noise from the tyres reverberated through the cab. She'd have to remember to fill them with air when she passed the next gas station but letting the air out always made a huge difference in the soft sand.

She turned her Jeep left at the campsite, spotted the entrance he'd mentioned and drove around the locked gate onto another dirt road. Although she'd visited this beach – even camped here a few times – she'd never noticed this track winding through the seaside scrub parallel to the beach. Now they climbed a grass-covered knoll.

On top and surrounded by smaller sand dunes stood a solid beach house made of sand-coloured wood. Because of the height of the knoll it overlooked the beach in both directions yet blended into the hills. Tufts of coarse beach grass and wind-bent coastal shrubs ringed it.

The house stood sturdily on stilts and looked a lot larger than Misty's idea of a shack. A wide veranda gazed out over the vista below and she parked the car in the shade beside a late model Range Rover. Steep steps led up to the door.

Ben's eyelashes rested on his cheeks and she touched his arm. 'Will you be able to get inside, Ben?'

'I'll be fine.' His lids lifted slowly to reveal aquamarine corneas, the blue of the waves she'd been fishing this morning, and just as mesmerizing. 'Are you okay?'

She smiled. His concern for her was sweet but unfortunately the brightness of his eyes made his pale cheeks even more concerning. 'I'll be better when you have a bit of colour in your face.'

The memory of him floating face down in the water resurfaced in all its horrific glory. How she'd almost been unable to hold him as the wave dragged him back. She recalled those vital few seconds when he'd not been breathing. Still couldn't believe she'd managed keep him alive.

This flesh-and-blood, breathing human being would

be dead if she hadn't been there.

That thought left her with a deep nausea that rose ominously. She shook her head. Battled an intense bout of the shivers as her stomach roiled.

'Excuse me,' she gulped, wrenching open her door to fall to the ground where at least she could be out of sight to throw up. 'Sorry.'

The soft word of self-reproach had not been intended to be heard. Yet he appeared, still swaying, beside her. With one hand on the car for support he scooped her ponytail from her face and held it behind her head while she completed the job.

For the moment she was too unwell to push him away. Or care.

'Poor brave mermaid.' His words soothed as his warm hand cupped her forehead offering comfort.

Misty shook her head. She wasn't brave. She'd been terrified. She could feel the prick of tears in her eyes as the nausea ran its course.

'I'm sorry.' She took his hand to help her to her feet and then she backed away from him. Wiped her mouth with the back of her hand and schooled any expression from her face.

Weakness when she was supposed to be in charge wasn't good.

But she'd have to let go of what had just happened, could cringe about it later, and changed the subject. 'I'm supposed to be nursing you.'

'I'm recovering. Thanks to you.' When she didn't look convinced he gestured wearily to the stairs. 'Come in. We'll both catch our breath. You can check me out when you're feeling better.'

Funny how he'd shifted his concern from himself to her and she felt the pull that shimmered around this Ben, this man she'd never met before, not in this lifetime. An awareness and recognition as if her heart was telling her something her head had to disbelieve. No idea what it meant.

Mentally she shrugged. She'd had years of weird feelings and this was just more of the same.

'Come with me,' he said, and the cadence of those simple words caught her as his long fingers caught her other hand. There it was. That recognition she'd noticed before.

It was as if his whole arm pulled her along not so much by his strength but by a magnetic attraction between them that shouldn't be there. Weakly, with her inner voice quietly insisting she was meant to be here, she followed him up the steps and into his house. Holding his hand.

INSIDE THE HOUSE, dark lacquered wood floors showcased several glowing rugs. Rectangular works of art that screamed ancient Persia and threw glorious splashes of colour against the darkness in delicate stitches. Rugs she wanted to lean down and lay her fingers against and stroke.

Odd-shaped chairs constructed from driftwood leaned around the walls, big but comfortable looking, and a huge, ancient seaman's chest used as a table stood covered with books.

The circular centre of the house had three other rooms leading off it. Ben drew her into one, a sunlit bathroom furnished like a shiny capsule from a luxury motor yacht, complete with a huge round tub that looked over the beach. Then he finally let her hand go.

She looked down and, incredibly, her fingers looked normal. She'd expected her skin where he'd touched to at least glow. No such fanciful complaint seemed to bother him as he passed her a fresh facecloth and towel.

'You'll find a new toothbrush in the top drawer. There.' He gestured toward a rustic dresser. 'I'll leave you to it.' Then he closed the door behind him and left.

Turning toward the mirror, Misty saw her pale and strained face and realised that he looked more recovered than she did now. Huh.

The mirror's incongruous frame caught her attention. Someone had surrounded the glass with a circle of inexpertly glued shells. Were these the shells from the vision? Did this mean she was meant to be here?

It didn't matter. She *was* here. And she'd made a fool out of herself by throwing up.

But it wasn't every day you came across a man face down in the water. And had to do mouth to mouth to start him breathing.

She tried not to think of what would have happened if she hadn't had the premonition, hadn't found the right headland so soon after he fell in, but she would never again even hint that she regretted her second sight.

That gift had saved this man's life and she would be forever grateful.

The cold tap water splashed against her heated cheeks helped restore normality. As she brushed her teeth Misty glanced once more at her reflection. Some colour had crept back into her face and she couldn't subdue the tiny flutter of satisfaction that all the years of her nurse's training had stood by her on the beach.

She'd saved a life.

As long as she remembered this was a moment out of time and not the real world, she could admit it was not how she'd seen her day panning out. Here she stood, looking into a mirror in a handsome stranger's beach house, and she couldn't deny there was a magnetism about the man that had her intrigued.

When she opened the bathroom door, the central room stood ominously empty. She glanced around, the worry returning that maybe Ben wasn't as well as he'd seemed a few minutes ago.

'In here.' His voice, from beyond another of the open doorways, sounded fatigued and her step quickened.

Ben sat on the edge of a wide white bed with a towel around his waist. She pulled her eyes and thoughts back from considering what lay underneath that towel, *what on earth was she thinking*, and looked at his face.

The profile from the vision now seemed carved in her mind.

Lines of angry abrasions crossed his chest and a trickle of blood skimmed his hairline. Her sensible side reasserted as she considered what needed to be done. She picked up a box of tissues from the dresser before she crossed the room to sink to her knees beside the bed.

She looked up into his face and narrowed her eyes.

Both pupils seemed equal and reactive when she shaded the light from the window. One, then the other again. Yep. Pupils reacting and equal in size. So far so good.

'How's your head?' She ran her fingers lightly over the

spongy swelling under his hairline, dabbed the blood away with a tissue, and he winced.

'Ouch,' she said in sympathy, but didn't pause as she continued her check. He'd have to put up with the discomfort because she needed to know if there was something worse to find.

'I can tell you're in the medical profession,' he murmured. 'Too much common sense.'

She grinned and palpated his scalp to ensure the bone didn't feel displaced underneath. The bump seemed slightly smaller already than when she'd first checked it on the beach. Her hand slid around the base of his skull to check for further injury and his ink-black hair felt distractingly soft and springy. The darn strands curled around her fingers as if welcoming her touch.

It seemed so long since she'd done that to a lover. She'd forgotten the sensation of running her fingers through a man's hair. Which wasn't a medically professional thought at all.

'From what I can tell you seem to have come out pretty well,' she said as she forced her fingers to untangle themselves from a warm and welcoming place they didn't want to leave. Where they did not belong.

'My head is improving all the time.' His voice held a whisper of weary teasing. 'Especially when you stroke it.'

Her hand bounced away as if scalded. When she met his eyes he smiled wryly at her reaction.

'The joker is back.'

'I'm sure I'll be fine,' he replied in a more serious tone. 'I'm cold and headachy. But I am curious to know your name.'

She balled the tissues she'd used and placed them on

the floor. Grabbed a new handful. 'Misty.' She nodded at his chest and looked at him for tacit permission before she touched it. The jagged scratches were red and welted but she couldn't see any pieces of shell in the wound and felt nothing jagged when she wiped the wounds. She flattened a clean tissue over the now dry wounds and felt the heat of inflammation.

'Look at your poor chest.' A sudden mad impulse to kiss his cheek in sympathy made her straighten away from him. She glanced at the bloody tissues in her hands and admonished herself. What on earth was the matter with her? This man was an unknown entity and after today she'd never meet him again.

She stood and nodded towards the en-suite she could see across the room. 'First aid in there?'

'Yes. And there's antibiotic powder on the shelf you could use.'

After washing her hands, she used more tissues to blot the seeping blood from his chest and then puffed the powder onto his wounds. She stood back and tried to think what else she could do for him, but her mind was suddenly blank so she returned the powder to the tiny bathroom and disposed of the waste.

When she returned at least she'd thought of something. 'Is your tetanus booster up to date?'

'Yes,' he supplied quietly, 'and a bump on the head and a few scratches are a small price to pay.' He patted the bed next to him. 'Sit for a minute. You're very safe. I think we both need reassurance.'

Misty found herself hip to hip with him and she had no idea how she'd got there as he slipped his arm around her shoulders and pulled her closer. She felt small under the weight of his arm yet the contact soothed her jangling nerves. They sat side by side, contemplating his lucky escape, and surprisingly she drew the comfort he had intended from the gesture.

She felt oddly at ease with this man whose life had hung so precariously in the balance that very afternoon, and with the slow warming of his skin against hers came the reinforcement of the knowledge of his survival. Satisfaction grew that this man

was here safe and firm against her and the world outside the house seemed a million miles away.

He turned and his mouth touched hers, warm and fleeting. 'Thank you,' he said simply. The kiss was over before she could avoid it, unlike the impact which lingered, pure and beautiful, like a note from a Tibetan bowl.

Her mouth vibrated with the memory and she mashed her lips together as if to blot the imprint out because the thrumming continued in decreasing waves.

'Thank you for saving my life, Misty.' His eyes were as blue as the ocean he'd come from and his gaze roamed her face as if he wanted to imprint her on his mind.

Time stopped and she could do nothing but stare back at him as his voice floated over her. Heat rose beneath her skin under his scrutiny and suddenly there was a clawing tumble of unbidden sensations in her belly.

Whoa there.

She blinked, broke eye contact and searched desperately for something to say. Something at least tinged with professionalism. Something like...

'Let me see your back.' Definitely not *let me see your backside.*

CHAPTER 4

Ben

Ben closed his eyes and twisted his body so she could see. Pushed away the flicker of frustration he had no right to feel.

At least one of them had their feet firmly on the ground. Perhaps it was a by-product of his concussion, but he was having difficulty concentrating on anything else but her beautiful mouth and luscious body pressed against his. This being a damn inappropriate time to start dreaming about what she would look like with her shirt off.

Then she touched his back with those slender mermaid's fingers and not being able to see her hands on him made it more frustratingly erotic than it should have been. He could imagine her leaving luminous trails on his skin, like phosphorescent lines in the water at night.

Desire stirred beneath the towel and he shifted uncomfortably as he turned and reached across to capture her hand and still her fingers. He looked down. Such long fingers as they lay in his. Such invisible strength within them.

She must have a heart as strong as a lioness. He had no doubt that was her secret.

There was something pure and powerful and golden about Misty that shone so brightly even someone as jaded as he could see her worth.

His grip tightened and unconsciously he inched her back to face him until their sides touched again. And then he froze. What was he doing?

His head ached, his chest hurt and he'd nearly died. He owed his survival to this woman. All the more reason to act on the moment, his inner demon suggested unhelpfully. He staunched that devil with determination that took almost more effort than he had.

He did not need another complication in his life and from the little he'd seen of her, he had no doubt this woman could be extremely complicating. That subtle air of naivety warned him he was the much more experienced of the two of them, but it also worried him.

'Thank you, Misty,' he said. 'I think you'd better go.'

Her eyes widened and he saw the moment she realised what he meant. Heat dusted her cheeks and she stood up quickly and looked around the room as if she'd forgotten where the exit was. He smiled at her disorientation, sympathetic because he'd suffered some recent confusion too at her hands, even as it showed him more than anything that he'd done the right thing to call a halt.

She could feel it, too, he thought.

He stood, intending to follow her to the door, when the room tilted away from him like the deck of a ship as it rode a swell. A rush of cold doused him and then nothing as he fell backwards.

Misty

Misty managed to reach out and guide him back onto the bed before he crumpled to the floor. But even lifting his muscled legs, one at a time, reminded her of the struggle she'd had to get him out of the water. He was, indeed, a big guy.

She bent to lift his lids but his eyes flickered open and he blinked groggily as he tried to sit up. His face shone like alabaster even in the dim room. 'What happened?'

'You fainted. I think you should stay down, Ben. I'll call an ambulance so they can check you out at the hospital.'

'No. I'll refuse to go.' He lifted his hand and rested it over his eyes. 'I don't need a hospital. It would be a wasted trip for emergency services when they could be saving someone else.'

Misty stared with wide, incredulous eyes. 'You are kidding me. Right?' God save her from stubborn men with more pride than good sense.

'That's ridiculous. You've lost consciousness twice from a head injury, had a respiratory arrest—' she ticked off his symptoms on her fingers '—and are probably brewing pneumonia. You need to be observed.'

Ben rubbed his forehead. 'I'm fine. I just need to sleep.'

Misty couldn't stop her hands going to her hips and she stood over him and glared. The man was exasperating. 'You might never wake up.'

He just looked at her.

He didn't look like he cared? Her eyes stung at this realisation and the reaction made her even more cross. 'Well, what a waste of energy and effort for me, today!'

'Thank you. You're saved my life, but I'm not going anywhere. Especially to a hospital!'

Finality rang in the last four words and Misty stamped her foot with frustration. He winced at the sharp sound and she pulled herself back under control. Her voice dropped to nurse-speak. 'Come on, Ben. Be sensible. I can't just leave you.'

He closed his eyes and blew out a breath. 'So observe me for another hour, or the four required, and then when you feel satisfied you can go. Or stay in the spare room and leave in the morning.'

Misty glanced at her watch. Four hours. It would be dark by then, but her swag was in the Jeep, along with all her clothes. She could leave tomorrow instead of today; what choice did she have? She did not want to read in the paper about a man found dead in an isolated beach house.

She looked around but there wasn't a chair in the room. Recent experience told her that sitting beside him on the bed was not the best idea. She'd drag in a chair from somewhere.

Ben had shifted up the bed to rest on the pillows while she'd been going over her options. Trying to read her face. 'So how did you stumble across me in my hour of need? The beach is usually deserted.'

Misty rarely spoke about her gift and she hesitated at sharing such a personal subject with a stranger. Now was not the time to get into a discussion that would probably end with Ben thinking her fanciful. Better she project her practical nursing side. 'Just luck.' She gestured toward the doorway and the living room beyond. 'I'll get a chair.'

Ben lifted his arm and pulled a pillow across from the pile beside him. Created a puffy barrier between them. His weary eyes twinkled despite his exhaustion.

'Here. Lie down next to me. I'll put a pillow-wall up to protect you.'

'I don't think so,' Misty said, and went in search of a seat. There was a huge old recliner in the next room that looked incredibly comfortable but it would never fit through the door into Ben's bedroom.

Then there were the driftwood chairs, lining the walls like fabulous works of art. But when she tried one out, the knobs and bends were in the most uncomfortable places.

She couldn't lounge on them for four hours.

The kitchen had high-backed bar stools and she sighed as she carried one through.

'That looks comfortable,' Ben said conversationally, but then he shook his head. 'I can't stand the thought of you perched up there just because you're a good Samaritan.' He looked thoughtful for a moment. 'It's really not been a good day for good Samaritans all round. I wouldn't have nearly drowned if I hadn't been trying to save a bird.'

Well at least he remembered that. A sign of no amnesia.

'I'll get up,' he decided. 'It's a step too far for you to suffer further on my account. We'll sit in the loungeroom.'

He was either incredibly well-mannered or incredibly sneaky, but she really had no choice if she wanted to be comfortable while keeping an eye on him. And now he was levering himself up, as if preparing to try standing again.

'For goodness' sake. Stay put. I'll lie down next to you. But don't blame me if I go to sleep. I've been driving since early this morning and spent a couple of hours in the sun this afternoon. It's a detour but I wanted to say goodbye to my favourite lighthouse.'

'Perfect. We'll both sleep.' He closed his eyes briefly, as if they stung.

She was glad to see his eyelids droop but then he began to speak again.

'My luck must have changed.' His eyes still shut. Then they opened and he said, quite seriously, as she lowered herself onto the bed as far away as possible from him. 'You have a way of making me forget all reason in the most disconcerting way.'

He smiled across at her, and it changed him into a much younger man, a less world-weary one, and for a moment her knees trembled and she was pathetically grateful she was lying and not standing because she might have collapsed, boneless, on top of him.

He closed his eyes and she managed to draw a discreet steadying breath and edge another inch further away from him. She hit a problem. She needed that pillow wall he'd talked about but she felt silly asking for it.

Still with his eyes shut, he shifted across the bed until their shoulders touched. His arm slid under and around her shoulders. Ben's hand was cool against her upper arm but under her skin heat rose up her body like black ink soaking into white chalk.

Once gathered the heat wasn't going anywhere. It just got warmer and warmer.

Ben's voice sounded sleepy. 'So, where have you driven from today and where're you going?'

Misty tried to focus on words not sensations. Anything to move her mind away from her other senses. Focus on the real world. That's a novel idea, she mocked herself, and organised her thoughts to answer his question.

'I'm moving to Lyrebird Lake to work in a birth centre with my brother and sister-in-law.'

'Lyrebird Lake?' Ben's interest seemed genuine. 'What does your brother do?'

She thought of her big, kind, brother. 'Andy is the GP running the small town hospital, but he doesn't have much to do with the birthing side. He married my best friend and they're expecting a new baby. She started the unit for women-centred care.' She heard the excitement in her voice. It was a project worth enthusing about. 'It will be the absolute best place to have a baby.'

He pulled a face. Still with eyes shut. 'Women-centred care?' Misty could see he was unfamiliar with the term. 'Define that?'

This was a wonderful diversion from the heat in her stomach. Misty could talk about this till the whales swam north. 'Each midwife has her own caseload of clients in order to better meet the needs of the mother. More focus gives more satisfaction all round.' She turned a little to face him. 'The idea is to give each woman holistic care that can cover all the facets of pregnancy from antenatal education, mental status, labour, breastfeeding and, of course, caring for baby when he or she comes home.'

Ben opened his eyes, stared at her as if he didn't get it. 'I know obstetrics, but this isn't familiar.' His voice held an extra dimension she couldn't quite place but he went on quickly as if speeding away from the topic he'd started and now regretted. 'Babies. New life.' Ben turned his head to stare at the ceiling. Said softly as if to himself, 'I wonder if what happened today means my slate is clean?'

The note of despair could have been imagined but something in his anguished profile tugged at Misty. 'I don't understand...'

'Can I begin a new life because I so nearly lost the old one?'

She studied the contours of his face for the time, soon, when she'd have to leave. 'I believe anyone can start a new life if they are determined.'

He turned to look at her and there was a glow in his eyes that made her catch her breath. 'Are you destined to change my life?'

'Unlikely when we'll probably never meet again.' Impossible dream. She lifted her hand and peered at her watch as if to remind herself she needed to leave in a few hours.

This was getting too personal. She tried to lighten the

mood. 'I doubt I'm destined to go around dragging you out of life-threatening situations, Ben.'

His arm tightened. The salty tang of the sea and Ben seemed to drift around her like the waves that had almost claimed him. 'But you saved my life so beautifully.'

The memories rushed back and she shivered. 'Don't joke about it, Ben, please. Today was very close.'

'Sorry.' He stilled and then squeezed her shoulder in comfort. 'Resuscitation is always frightening. I'm sorry you had to do that, Misty.'

She forced her mind away from those indelible pictures and closed the subject with finality. 'I think you're safe enough for me to get up now.'

'So, you're a midwife,' he mused, ignoring her statement. His voice was low, slow, enthralling. 'That would explain the mothering you've been doing.'

Her neck ached from trying to maintain some distance from his encircling arm, and she gave up. She rested back into the pillow and stared rigidly at the ceiling. Blinked.

Stars were glued to shape constellations above the bed. The constellations looked to scale. There was Scorpio and Sagittarius and Gemini. How amazing. She imagined they would glow fabulously at night. It would have taken days to create.

He had too much time on his hands if he'd been making sky art and mirror frames and driftwood chairs, although that was none of her business. She tried to remember what he'd said, while she'd been side-tracked by the star signs...

Oh, yes, midwives and mothering.

He gave a short mirthless laugh and she was jolted out of her contemplation. 'In my time—' his voice held self-contempt and she frowned at the disruption to the ambience in the room '—I worked with women but nothing like you've spoken about. It was in another lifetime and I don't think I could ever go back.'

'You're an obstetrician, then?' That would explain his midwife comment.

'Was.'

'How do you stop being that when you're as young as you are?'

She let the words lie between them because something told her she'd been privileged to hear even that information. It seemed she'd done the right thing because he went on as if the words were forced out of him. 'I'll never go back.'

She had to ask. 'Why?'

He breathed deeply. 'Everyone has bad runs. It's funny how something you would normally accept as a tragedy of nature can overwhelm you unexpectedly. Something happened and I lost it. That's all.'

Misty had seen her fair share of sadness, but, then, she'd always felt that dealing with loss in midwifery was something you shared with parents as a brief moment to hold onto for the future. A privilege and an honour if you were the one to help them steer through the deep and despairing waters of loss and fleeting parenthood. 'I guess it depends on your own life experience how things can affect you.'

'You don't know how true that is,' he said, and the words seemed to be dragged from a place deep inside him. Misty decided she wouldn't offer any more comments in case she caused further pain. Silence was something she could be good at.

The quietness stretched and Misty waited for his cue. He might change the topic or continue to share. It was his call.

After what seemed like an eternity, she eased her fingers into his palm and wrapped her hand around his, to at least let him know she was aware of his hurt. At her tentative offer of comfort his hand tightened in surprise and then, very slowly, his fingers relaxed in hers.

Strange how much it meant that he hadn't pushed her away. Seemed he wasn't used to people offering him comfort and it made her want to pull his head down onto her chest and stroke his beautiful hair. But she couldn't do that.

She didn't even know this man. And yet she felt she knew him better than many people she'd spent weeks or months working beside.

Eventually Ben raised his head and made a short, bitter sound of amusement. 'Imagine you wanting to comfort me.'

'I don't find that funny,' Misty said quietly.

He turned to look at her. His smile softened, lost its cynical edge. 'No, you wouldn't. Because you, dear Misty, are a real person and I haven't seen your like for a very long time.'

She let go of his hand but not his gaze. 'Probably because you live in a beach house on a deserted beach,' she said dryly. 'You haven't seen any people. You should get out more.'

'Actually, I've done all I need to do with my life. I've written a text on postnatal depression and achieved all I was going to achieve. You should probably have left me to drown.'

Misty felt his words like a vicious jab to the stomach and she drew in a breath. She wanted to punch his arm. 'Don't ever speak like that again,' she said fiercely. She leaned up on one elbow and stared down into his face and glared ferociously, suddenly livid with him. He looked world-wearily amused, but she didn't care. This was important. 'Every life is precious.'

She pulled herself free of him and sat her back high up on the pillows. 'It is sad not all patients can be saved, but you have been!' She poked him with one finger. 'By me, and that gives me some rights to tell you so. There is a desperate need for skills like yours out in this world. How dare you just fritter them away like a wastrel in your beach house?'

It was probably all the stress of the day, she could have almost died too, and suddenly she was so angry she could barely draw breath. 'You were given a new chance at life today, a chance you nearly didn't have. One of the mysteries of the universe is how I found you.' She poked him again. 'I could have drowned trying to save you so don't you even think of letting me down.'

Misty subsided, finally, but she could feel her heart pounding with the agitation of her emotions. She didn't know this man, this person she'd just lectured like some prissy know-it-all, but maybe saving his life did give her some rights because it had needed saying, but now it was horrible because she felt the tears welling as she tried to calm down.

Ben sighed. Pulled himself up next to her. Took back her hand. 'I'm sorry, Misty. I was being irresponsibly flippant. Everything you say is right. It was a glib and silly comment and I do regret upsetting you.'

It was his turn to look down into her face. She hoped he couldn't see the tears at the corners of her eyes because suddenly she felt weepy and miserable, no doubt from the huge emotions of the day, but it was embarrassing nonetheless.

Of course Ben noticed.

He turned her towards him and gathered her close to encircle her body with his arms. 'I'm sorry, mermaid.'

He pulled her even closer until their cold noses touched. She could feel his bare skin between them, from her breasts to her hips and again at the knees, and his eyes stared into hers, intense and questioning. And so very blue.

'Where have you come from?' Their noses rubbed as he pushed his face against hers. 'Why couldn't I have met you when I was young and idealistic, like you?' He shook his head, hair flying, as if it was all beyond his understanding. 'How can there be such emotion and connection between two strangers?'

She knew just what he meant. 'I don't know,' she whispered as she watched him wince at the discomfort of too much head shaking.

'I don't understand either, Misty, but I'm very, very grateful.' His deep mumur caressed her, soothing the brittle edges of her distress. 'Thank you for saving my life and putting your precious life at risk to do that. I will always value your gift. Now, hush. It's okay.'

He kissed away the dampness from her cheeks, feather-touched the end of her nose with his mouth, and finally settled his firm lips on hers. And then it all merged.

He was the mysterious man she'd dreamt of in her bed late at night and never imagined she would really meet.

He pulled back to stare, perplexed and startled at the connection that seared between them, then his breath merged seamlessly with hers again as he kissed her until it felt as if their very souls touched. Here was a place she'd known she had but had never dared to visit.

CHAPTER 6

Ben

Ben drew Misty so close he could feel his heart pound in time to hers. His eyes never left her gentle face as he drew away.

'Rest. We'll both rest,' he said and lay back to stare at the stars on the ceiling, willing his body to let it go. Let her go. 'It's been a big day.'

What was he doing? Back off, Ben admonished himself as he relaxed his head back on the pillow. She'd saved his life and he was taking again.

But what the hell had just happened? He screwed his eyes shut and relaxed his shoulders into the bed. Shifted slightly so he was very gently touching hers. Savoured the tiny connection.

. . .

SURPRISINGLY THEY BOTH SLEPT. When Ben woke up it was dark outside and Misty lay spooned against him like a kitten. He felt so much better, and disturbingly aroused.

Misty's soft, sleeping face sent a spasm of tenderness into his heart that had nothing to do with her saving his life. They must have turned at some time in their sleep like an old married couple spooning with chastity, an old married couple who'd never consummated their marriage. He grinned in the darkness.

Well, that was a first with a beautiful woman in his bed.

And she was beautiful, this fierce little mermaid who'd saved his life and refused to leave him alone. Her red hair tumbled around her sweet features and kissable mouth. If only he was a better man.

He touched her silken cheek and then slid away before his body found more bright ideas. Closed the ensuite door before she woke up and enticed him beyond reason. She wouldn't have to do much.

He planted his hands on the sink and stared into the mirror. His eyes stared back sardonically. *Down, boy.*

Speaking of which, the swelling had almost gone from the bump on his head. His chest scrapes looked angry in interesting stripes but dry from the antibiotic powder Misty had applied. When he peered into his eyes his pupils seemed equal, and he wasted a couple of seconds trying to see the dilation response before he frowned at the hopelessness of trying to catch a pupil reaction on his own face. Idiot. Of course he couldn't. But anything to stop his mind wandering back into the bedroom next door.

'Are you OK, Ben?' Misty's voice came through the

door and he glared into the mirror to warn himself to behave.

She was supposed to sleep for another hour. Give him time to think. 'Fine, thanks. Be out in a sec,' he said. 'Right after the freezing shower,' he finished under his breath. And turned on the cold tap.

WHEN HE OPENED the bathroom door five minutes later she'd straightened the bed and disappeared. He found her on the dark veranda, gazing out over the beach. The sliver of moon was just rising, but the sky was lightening on the horizon where it would emerge.

'It's beautiful when the full moon rises at night out of the sea,' he said as he stopped beside her and slipped his arm around her shoulders. Her neck was taut under his hand and as he rubbed that tender curve he noticed the nervousness she'd acquired now she'd remembered they were strangers.

Well, that was fair enough. Very wise of her. She should be having second thoughts on her decision to stay.

Reluctantly, his arm slid from her shoulders and he stepped back. He could still feel her warmth against his body, delicate though it was, and he seriously wanted her back against him.

She squeezed her hands over her upper arms as if to warm herself and he jammed his hands into his trouser pockets.

No doubt she had some boyfriend to rush off to, or she could even be married with kids. He smiled to himself at that. She wore no ring. He'd checked that while holding her as they'd drifted off to sleep.

Now, why had he done that?

He needed space between them or he'd be working to initiate something he couldn't finish. Something they'd both regret. 'Would you like a drink?' He turned, gesturing vaguely toward the house inside.

She nodded with ridiculous enthusiasm, making him aware the strain sat both sides. 'Do you have juice?' she asked as she followed him back into the kitchen. Even though she walked behind him he could pinpoint her position.

How odd. It had never been like that before. Ever.

This mysterious, amazing young woman who had swum into his life, saved him, scolded him, and captured his imagination when he'd least expected it might prove rather difficult to forget.

'Your "shack" is impressive,' she said in that warm way she had, but there seemed a fragile brightness to her face as her eyes skittered away from his. Was it because they'd slept so easily together? Such an incongruous thing for strangers to do.

Enough regret. Stop being self-indulgent, he mocked himself, and forced his voice to lightness. He'd give her a drink and she'd be ready to leave.

'If you want to see something really impressive, come and see my refrigerator. I indulged myself and bought the biggest I could get.' He'd been avoiding having to shop. 'What type of juice would you like?'

She peered at the selection like a kid in an ice-cream parlour. 'Hmm...decisions, decisions.'

Ben savoured her vacillation. Couldn't help the smile in his voice. 'You could have two different juices if you really wanted.'

She darted a startled look at him, embarrassed. Her pale skin blushed easily. Of course, being a natural redhead. He remembered how her cheek had felt like silk under his fingers, just like the rest of her. He lifted his hand to reach her.

'Mango juice, thanks.' She grabbed the bottle and turned away so that his hand fell away.

Ben sighed and closed the wall-sized chrome door and leaned his forehead against the cold steel for a moment. What was he doing? Don't touch her again, you idiot, he thought. Closed his eyes. The last thing he wanted was to hurt someone again and his life was as complicated as ever.

He needed to tell her to go.

That he'd be fine.

That it would be better for her if she left.

He opened his eyes and turned to do it. She wasn't there. The room lay empty and the juice stood unopened on the sea chest. He walked through to the veranda. She wasn't there either and he scanned the stairs.

The unmistakable sound of her vehicle door closing echoed the emptiness he hadn't realised she'd leave behind. He'd always had that emptiness. It hadn't mattered before. Did he really want to be alone?

The engine came to life , light flooded the yard, and he had no control over his feet as they turned to the stairs. Taking them two, three, at a time. The next thing he knew he was beside her Jeep window. 'Stay with me,' he said. The noise of the engine between them. Gazes locked. Seconds passed. She didn't reverse away and he began to hope.

He recognised the moment she acknowledged the

temptation, searched his face for reassurance, and considered staying. He swore to himself he wouldn't let her down if she did. She was unique. Different. He couldn't believe that he was daring to dream again.

His fingers reached through the window of their own accord and turned the key.

Made it happen.

Though she still had the choice.

The engine died.

Silence surrounded them, except for the pounding of waves on the shore and the squawk of gulls overhead... And the hammering in his heart.

She looked at him with those glorious witch's eyes of hers and he could feel himself drowning, which was ironic considering what the previous day had held.

He held out his hand. 'Stay with me. Please.' Heard the quiet hope in his own voice.

Misty raised her hand towards his and then stopped. Looked away. 'What are you asking, Ben?'

'To come back in.'

'I know what will happen if I go back into the house with you. I might even want it to happen. But we need to think sensibly about this. Safely and non-emotionally. It's an impossible dream. We both have lives, and commitments, and uncertainties, and we met this once by the merest chance.' She lifted her fingers to the ignition and turned the key. 'I don't think so. Take care, Ben.'

'You, too.'

She glanced once more at his face and the expression suddenly stripped from her features as if someone had turned off a light.

Right decision, Ben thought. Sensible girl.

. . .

SHE WAS GONE and Ben lay alone in his big bed with just the scent of her skin on the pillow beside him and emptiness in his heart as he said goodbye. Sensible, sensible girl.

The sound of a ringtone filled the room.

His phone.

His breath shuddered in his throat as he sat up, and he shook his head at the person on the other end. 'I'll come,' he said into his phone.

He looked out the window at the rolling ocean and his chin lifted. Impossible dream, he thought, uncannily echoing Misty as he shut his phone and reached for his shirt.

CHAPTER 7

Misty

$\mathcal{M}$isty didn't remember much about the drive to Lyrebird Lake. Barely saw Coffs Harbour as she drove past it again, not noticing her old stamping ground before she turned west. The memory of Ben Moore, in her rear-view mirror watching her go, just seemed to get bigger the further away that she drove. She needed to leave to start her new life before he imprinted further on her soul.

But had she missed a singular opportunity? Had Ben been the man for her to experience life and love with? Had he been the one man for her?

More likely a one-night stand with someone who obviously moved fast, although it would certainly have been memorable. She had no doubt about that.

He didn't even know her last name.

. . .

SHE STAYED the night at a motel, couldn't remember which town as soon as she drove away the next morning. It had been hard to get up and drive further west into Queensland. Now, hours later, as she passed through the wide and tree-lined streets of Lyrebird Lake, her spirits began to lift. She'd saved a life. That was the important thing to take away from her brief encounter with Ben Moore.

It was time to start here fresh. Like Ben needed to. She hoped he'd find happiness some day.

She turned her Jeep into the driveway of her brother's house, sighing deeply as she reached over to turn off the engine. She'd done the right thing. She *had*.

The big door opened and 'Welcome to Lyrebird Lake,' floated out as her sister-in-law rushed towards her. Misty heard the words and accepted the hug Montana offered.

It was wonderful to see her best friend again but there was no doubt the excitement of her moving to the same town as Andy and best friend had been affected by meeting Ben.

She hoped Montana didn't notice the effort it took to smile.

Her big brother's arms came around her and were just what she needed to make her feel strong again. 'I bet you didn't see this in our future.' Andy laughed as he hugged her.

'There were a lot of things I didn't see,' she said and tried to smile.

Andy held her away from him and frowned at her searchingly. 'What's happened to you?'

'Shh, love,' Montana said, and Misty watched with wry

amusement as her friend rested her hand on Andy's arm. 'Let your sister get her breath. We have plenty of time.'

'Assuming the phone doesn't ring and I don't get called out,' Andy muttered, as he carried Misty's bags into their house.

She followed with her arm hooked in Montana's. The two women shared a glance and smiled. Poor Andy, the look said, he hated to miss out and they both loved his care. 'He's still looking for a locum to share the workload because he won't let me out of his sight until I have this baby,' Montana whispered.

'Well, you were alone last time you had a baby.'

Montana, a widow at the time of her first baby's birth two years ago, had been alone at a mountain retreat when labour had begun rapidly without warning. Unable to drive any further, Montana had pulled over before she could reach the hospital, and at sunrise had delivered her daughter alone on an escarpment with only a wallaby to watch over her.

One of Misty's premonitions had urged her brother to search for and find Montana and her new baby. Andy had found more than the two people he'd been looking for. He had found his love.

This time Montana's birth experience would be different because Andy would be there for her. Misty was here too, now, and she would keep Montana safe as well.

Half an hour later Misty could feel the healing from the sense of family and love around her, and she began to relax as she eased into the rhythm of the household. The three of them were seated on the veranda of Montana and Andy's newly built home and the outdoor sail overhead shaded them from the fierce Queensland sun. The breeze from the lake stirred the air with tantalising wisps of coolness.

The weather in inland Queensland weather differed from her previous home on the north coast of New South Wales, but she'd acclimatise to the heat. She would. And grow used to the lack of access to the ocean... But how much of that was the ocean or the fact that the intriguing Ben resided there? She'd done the right thing to choose the stability of family and Lyrebird Lake over the uncertainty of a man who'd briefly touched her life. No matter that the touch had been so iridescent across all planes.

Misty glanced inwards to the open-plan house, a sprawling building of light and

large windows all shaded by verandas. It made her think of another house with polished floorboards and a different kind of heat. 'Your house is beautiful and yet it's very much a home.'

Andy smiled indulgently. 'Wait until Dawn wakes up. Our daughter can demolish it in minutes.'

'Imagine the chaos when her new brother or sister arrives.' Misty glanced at Montana's rounded stomach. 'You'll have twice as much mess to clean up.'

Her two favourite people in the world exchanged loving glances and she stifled a sigh. If only it were that easy. But then, those two hadn't had it easy either. She found some comfort in that.

'So tell me who broke your heart and I'll go and wring his neck.' The concerned look on Andy's face brought a hiccough of laughter and a sting of tears to her eyes.

So something showed. And she thought she'd been hiding her distraction.

Andy had always looked after her, always cared and

worried that his little sister was okay, especially after their mother had died. But Misty had been able to read his mind for years. She knew he worried she'd avoided relationships in case her gift spoilt them. She'd wondered if being married would change that care, but obviously not.

The prickle of tears in her throat itched. 'What makes you think my heart is broken? And why does it have to be a man?'

Andy blinked and she laughed with only a trace of bitterness at his confusion.

'Yes, it's a man,' she said before he bogged down in some, improbable for her, scenario.

'You waited all this time to find someone,' Andy tilted his head 'and then you moved? Why couldn't you have waited a bit longer until you got here? Found love at the lake and settled for good.'

Yes, Andy would like that. Montana would too. Fat chance, now, the way she felt at the moment. 'Give me time.'

'Is there a possibility for it all to work out?' Montana's quiet voice questioned, and Misty looked at her friend before she shook her head.

'Doubt it.'

'All what?' Andy looked between the women. 'You two are having conversations I can't hear.'

Misty smiled. 'Just a chance meeting and connection.'

Misty compared the understated wealth of the beach house to her modest finances, Ben's world-weary experience to her girlish optimism, her passion for birth and Ben's revulsion for obstetrics, and finally the fact that she hadn't even told him her surname. She had no doubt they would remain platonic ships in the night.

'It wouldn't have worked out,' she told Montana. 'No chance.' And accepted the finality with a new stab of loss. 'If he'd been less a man of the world, if we'd had a little more in common, he would have been perfect. It was also far too intense for stability, just a fantasy, and I was kidding myself.'

'I'm sorry.' Montana blew her a kiss that held understanding.

She looked at Montana. Felt again the touch of Ben's hand on hers. Shivered somewhere deep inside. 'It was so strange, though. The moment we met I felt a shift, as if I'd suddenly realised I'd only ever been half of myself. It's all a bit raw and of course I will survive.' She lifted her chin. 'But with him I felt I could achieve anything. In a strange way he made me feel like a queen.'

'Of course, you can still achieve anything! And you've always been a queen to me,' Andy said gruffly.

Montana reached across and squeezed Andy's hand. 'That's why I love your brother. My beautiful soulmate.' She smiled at her husband and then back at Misty. 'The attraction must have been potent to affect you like this.'

Misty raised her eyes. Said out loud what she'd been thinking on the drive. 'I left Coffs Harbour normal and arrived up here a totally different person. He changed me in just a few hours and I'll probably never see him again. The impact he's had on me is ridiculous.'

Andy rubbed the back of his neck as he searched for the right words. 'Let me get this straight. On the way here you had a one-night stand with some bloke you'd never met before and he's changed you forever?' Andy shook his head. 'And he didn't make arrangements to see you again?'

Misty sighed. 'It wasn't quite that simple and I didn't have a one-night stand.'

Andy's face lightened. 'At least that's good news.'

'Andy, love.' Montana patted her husband's hand. 'Stop playing bossy big brother and let Misty talk.'

All the wishing in the world didn't change the facts but Misty blew a kiss to her brother for his championing. 'We met under exceptional circumstances. We never had the chance to find out where it could go.'

'Why not?' Montana asked quietly.

It was unlike Montana to persist. It was as if she understood that

Misty needed to come to grips with what had happened. In some masochistic way it helped to confirm it had been nothing more than a dream. 'There was no future in it. Our stars collided for a day and that was all.'

'It must have been some collision,' her brother growled.

She looked at Montana. 'He was knocked off the rocks into the sea, and when I arrived, he'd almost drowned. I pulled him to shore and he wasn't breathing.'

'You risked your life for this guy?' Andy sat up straight, appalled his sister had been in danger.

'Always so fearless, Misty.' Montana understood and her calm voice soothed her husband into silence. 'But that must have been horrible.'

Too easily she could recall Ben's lifeless body on the beach. Misty shivered at the memory, rocking slightly as she continued. 'I had my body board. But even now I can still see him. Not breathing.'

Andy looked as though he approved of Ben's lifeless body and she swallowed an inappropriate giggle. As a big brother he was sweetly protective, but he didn't understand. If only life were that simple.

'All I know about him is that he lives on the beach and wrote a textbook.' She avoided mention of Ben's profession in case Andy knew him.

Her brother nodded his head. 'Of course,' he said sarcastically. 'He's self-indulgent and can't swim. And he preys on good Samaritans. Sounds like a hero to me.'

Misty laughed at her brother's simplistic image. 'He'd have swum if he hadn't been knocked out on the rocks, which I might add was after he saved a bird.'

Andy crossed his arms. 'Then he's clumsy as well.'

The two friends looked at each other, choosing to ignore Andy's final judgement.

'He's found you once,' Montana said. 'He'll find you again.'

'Thank you, Montana,' Misty said as she glanced at a scowling Andy. 'Unlikely that will happen, but thank you.'

CHAPTER 8

Ben

Ben climbed the rocks under the lighthouse, but all he could think of was a month ago and the sweet taste of Misty. The sweetness of her scent and the feel of her softness against him replayed every night in his bed. Too many memories snuck into his daylight hours as well.

Somehow, Misty had created a change in him, cracked his hard shell that barred the world. Misty had been brave and strong and quick-thinking and he'd been fighting against his instincts to follow and find her ever since.

The fact that he didn't know where she was at that moment was of no concern. He could find her at that lake she'd spoken about so passionately. The Lyrebird one. He had enough clues if he decided to go looking.

But would it be fair to her? Hadn't she done enough?

Too much to ask Misty to change the downward spiral of his life. His world was such a mess.

He ran his hand over the uneven surface of the cliff as if he'd find the answer there. Frustrated with his swirling thoughts he picked up a loose stone and spun it out over the waves towards the sunrise.

Of course it wasn't sensible to follow Misty. He tried to move on and forget her but even walking in his favourite place in the world didn't help. Every emerald-green rock pool reminded him of her. Every swirl of seaweed splayed and dipped like Misty's passion-red hair in the water.

Maybe he'd imagined the connection between them?

Could the peace he'd glimpsed with her be possible, even now he still hankered to find out? Could two people be spiralled into the almost mystical connection and not end up together again?

His life was even more complicated now than it had been then. She didn't need his problems and he didn't believe in fairy-tales. But he wanted her more each day.

Ben watched the water slap against the barnacles on the breakwall and considered knocking his stupid head against them. Forget her. He had responsibilities here now.

In the last month he'd been sorting the flotsam of disasters that had been drowning him even more than the sea had on the day Misty had appeared.

Tammy needed him and he'd help her as much as he could. Of course he would. Would Misty understand that even when Tammy wasn't his biological daughter she was still his beloved child?

Now that Tammy had asked for help he could do

something. Be there for her, when he'd been shut out before.

After her mother's death, he'd wanted Tammy to come and live with him, at least until she finished school. He'd offered to move somewhere, anywhere, so she could start again fresh and innocent of the worry her mother had heaped on her young shoulders in the months before she'd died.

But Tammy had stayed with her grandmother, had said Nanna needed her more, and now she was secretly pregnant. Lord knows how she had managed to hide that at almost eight months along, but the school knew now. Tammy had to leave in her second-last year, just like her mother had done seventeen years before and her grandmother had asked him for help.

Tammy needed to get away from the crowd she'd fallen in with. She refused to name the father of his grandchild but she'd agreed to ask for Ben's help in providing a safe harbour.

She wouldn't come to an isolated beach house.

He and Tammy needed to move... Somewhere.

Away.

He was so tempted to say Lyrebird Lake. He had Misty's word that it was the best place for any woman to have her baby. Surely Misty could help his confused and bitter young stepdaughter at the end of her pregnancy? She was a midwife. Maybe she could help them both.

But was it fair to Misty?

Misty

From the first, the tiny Lyrebird Lake Hospital and its midwifery unit welcomed Misty Buchanan with open arms.

That warm inclusion helped salve Misty's ache after the extraordinary effect of that day with Ben and the emptiness left in its wake.

Unlike a maternity unit in a larger hospital, Lyrebird Lake ran on a caseload of antenatal women with uncomplicated pregnancies. The town had accepted this new service with heartfelt relief from the only previous option. That had been a hospital stay eighty kilometres away from their families and the fragmented shared care they'd received there.

For the midwives there was a rewarding completion in the circle of care in their little hospital.

Of course, any complicated pregnancies or births were assessed by Andy or a locum doctor and transferred to the larger hospital at the base by ambulance for obstetric intervention. Even then, once stable, the woman and her baby could return to the lake prior to discharge home if she wanted to. Once home she'd connect with her midwife again.

Each midwife established a close rapport with her own clients and both sides were reluctant to change carers once the connections were made. So, Misty buddied with Montana and they'd worked so much together in the past that their styles melded easily. To avoid a gap in service when Montana went on maternity leave, Misty took over as much as she could so Montana could finish up without feeling she'd deserted her clients.

Everything smooth and ordered and she'd been almost settled after a month... Until last night.

The needs of the town had grown considerably with the local coal mine now in full operation, and the workload continued to increase. The mine's new housing estate had opened on the shores of the lake, ensuring the midwifery unit functioned more days than it was closed. Babies arrived calmly and naturally and then, tucked in their mother's or father's arms, sailed serenely out the door to go home.

Montana, who'd set up the unit with Andy's blessing and support, became one of Misty's own caseload clients when Charlotte, one of the other two midwives, handed over her care to Misty, although she would remain the back-up carer.

'This mother, Montana, is due in four weeks.' Charlotte grinned at her former client. 'She's very easy to get along with. It's her second baby and she has great resource skills for birth.'

Charlotte ceremoniously handed over the file and Misty laughed. 'I did hear she can be a little reluctant to come in when she starts labour, though.'

Misty glanced at Montana, who rolled her eyes. 'Very funny, you two. I assure you I am coming in this time. Andy has the car at the ready and never lets me out of his sight.'

In fact, Andy had come to take Montana home on her last day and he gathered her close to him with a soft smile. 'Ready to finally take it easy,' he said as he took Montana's bag from her to carry.

'So, you have your wife home for a while,' Misty teased her brother and he grinned back.

'Such a hardship.'

'You'll really hate being called out now.'

'I've got a locum,' Andy said smugly, and Montana and Misty both looked at him in surprise.

That had been sudden, Misty thought, and her stomach suddenly clutched with a mix of premonition and nerves.

'This guy is actually an obstetrician,' Andy supplied. 'Rang out of the blue and offered to start today. The paperwork's through and clear.'

'That seems a bit eager.' Montana sounded surprised, but then she couldn't hide her delight that her husband would have a lessened workload.

'Does this eager beaver have a name?' Misty tried to keep her voice nonchalant, but the wobble was there for her to hear, at least. Although she knew without asking, she had to check.

'Ben Moore. A widower. He's been out of obstetrics for a couple of years but we don't do obstetrics here anyway, do we, girls?' Andy teased them back. 'We have normal births. He's coming tomorrow.'

It was good to see her brother so happy, Misty told herself as a flutter of skittish seagulls, reminiscent of another day, flocked to her stomach. Of course, dear Andy had jumped at the chance to be able to spend more time with Montana at the end of her pregnancy. It was crazy to feel trapped and nervous when the news was so good for her brother but...

Ben was coming to the lake and she didn't think it was coincidence. Had he been as confused about their connection as she had? And done something about it.

It had been a month and she'd been congratulating herself that it had been a silly thing she had for him. Now this turned everything on its head.

THE NEXT MORNING, her first day in charge of maternity at Lyrebird Lake, Misty kept busy on the phone with the pregnant women on her caseload. She didn't have time to dwell on Ben's imminent arrival and what that meant.

All the time though, at the back of her mind, anticipation refused to behave itself. He'd come to find her. Or, her prosaic self said, he has another reason to be here. Andy had said Ben would arrive 'some' time today. What time, for goodness sake?

What would she say?

And what would he say? At least he couldn't say she'd been chasing him.

Why now when she'd finally started to think of him

less often? Could it possibly be a coincidence he'd decided to come, just when Andy needed him, or had he followed her?

She sniffed. It was no coincidence and she had no idea what he had in mind.

She needed less speculation and more concentration on the job.

But despite all the sensible reminders she couldn't completely dampen the flicker of hope that he'd followed her with a view to getting to know her better.

AN HOUR later when the door down the hall opened to the little maternity wing, Misty's hand stilled as she bent to tuck the end of the clean sheet under the mattress.

Was it him?

Already?

She wasn't prepared enough, and she looked around frantically as if she could find somewhere to hide.

Stop it! Misty breathed out and waited, calmly, she assured herself, for whoever was about to enter to close the door, and find her.

She forced herself to resume her task but in that frozen moment of intrusion it was strange how all her senses seemed to have come alive.

Time slowed to aching fragments of seconds and the tiny work-worn creases in her hands seemed suddenly enlarged and ugly when she stared down at her fingers. She could clearly identify the tang of bleach on the crisp, white hospital sheet and feel the slight stiffness in the cotton as it slid coldly beneath her fingers.

In slow motion she squared the corner of the sheet

and tucked it under the mattress before she straightened and strained her ears for more sound. The expected hail from her visitor didn't come. Only the world outside the windows drifted in, the passing cars, the call of birds, a scratchy rustle of a branch against the wall outside the room.

No footsteps? She frowned. Was it just someone lost? Come to the wrong doorway?

'Hello.' Her voice sounded much more uncertain than she'd expected. 'Who's there?' she called, and for a split-second Ben's arrival seemed less certain and a nasty alternative occurred to her. She began to edge back against the wall and unconsciously her hand slid protectively across her heart.

Finally the door swung closed again and then she heard the footsteps she'd been waiting for. Purposeful, not threatening or sinister. Somebody who was looking for a midwife, most likely, and her shoulders dropped with relief.

'Hello yourself.' The cadence echoed her own memory of Ben's voice and she let the sound wash over her with unexpected relief. 'I thought no one was here,' he said.

Ben wasn't the sinister intruder she'd conjured up in her imagination and she took a step towards him before she remembered a month had passed since she'd spoken to him last. And she didn't know why he was here.

Ben must have seen the tension on her face because his eyes narrowed as he glanced around. 'Misty? Are you okay?'

She sighed, heavily, still faint with tension. 'It's you.'

He tilted his head and his gaze roamed over her face,

as if reimprinting her on his memory. 'Who else did you think it might be?'

'No idea. Just had a silly fright. My nerves are shot,' she said, your fault, and laughed shakily before she dragged her eyes away from the intensity of his.

Ben Moore looked so large and vital and handsome and so different. Clean shaven, his once-unruly hair cut ruthlessly short.

It had been a little over a month since she'd seen him but in that time she'd grown so accustomed to recalling his bare chest in her mind's eye that she was startled by his tailored clothes. The white of his shirt shone brightly against the tan of his neck, and his forearms looked strong and brown under the rolled-up sleeves. The fitted design of his buttoned shirt complemented the breadth of his chest far too effectively and she looked away and then down at his feet.

Shoes. Definitely not bare, they were encased in expensive Italian loafers and topped by tailored grey trousers that made her think of city specialists, not locum country doctors. She wondered suddenly how he'd find working in an environment so different from that of a city hospital.

He looked… Out of her reach.

How could she tell this stranger she'd been thinking of him day and night for a month?

His eyes crinkled. 'I didn't think you had nerves,' he teased. He stepped closer. 'Your face is pale,' he said, and just that sympathy made her want to lay her head on his chest, and when he reached across to stroke her cheek, the single touch evoked the morning at the beach house in full sensory force. And all her weakness for a man she barely knew.

She jumped at the heat that transmitted itself through her skin from this strange Ben. A surge of warmth spread across her face and neck like a flash fire. Her brain urged her back against the wall and thankfully the plaster was cold enough against her spine to combat the conflagration that was spreading under the surface of her skin.

With her obvious recoil Ben's hand drew back and froze in mid-air before he tucked it in his pocket out of sight as if ashamed of the contact.

'I'm sorry.' He widened the gap between their bodies. 'Just pleased to see you.'

With a further step back, he glanced around as if seeing the room for the first time.

The silence stretched between them and Misty couldn't remember a time when she'd felt more uncomfortable. Or less able to find anything to fill the awkward pause.

Finally Ben spoke. 'So, no patients in here?' His comment hung, superfluous, in the empty ward, but at least he'd tried to fill the gap in conversation and she gestured to the half-made bed.

'I've just discharged the last.' Great help with the dialogue, she mocked herself, but that was all she could manage. She was too busy trying to control the thudding in her chest.

The silence lengthened and then his voice drifted softly across from where he stood. 'I'm sorry, Misty.'

She tilted her chin and met his gaze. Finally she had control. 'For what, Ben?' Her tone was cool. 'I'm the one who left.'

'For pressuring you when I shouldn't have.' He glanced around the empty room again. 'Can we talk about that?'

She knew he could see the barriers she'd erected so it was a silly question, but still his asking shocked her. 'Not here or now, no!'

'Oh?'

She looked around the empty ward. 'We may not have any inpatients at the moment, but this is a work place,' she said with quiet dignity. 'I'm a professional and won't bring that discussion to my work environment.'

Ben

Ben felt like slapping himself. 'No. Of course.' Stupidity. 'I'm sorry. But later?'

The woman would drive him mad with the way she looked at him as if she'd never felt any connection between them. But he could feel it vibrating between them like a wall of nerve endings, clacking in the breeze, like branches against a window.

She was right. He needed to ignore the sensations. Be the professional she wanted him to be. Pretend the connection wasn't there. She could do it, obviously.

After all, he'd come here for his daughter.

Not for Misty.

He'd keep telling himself that and eventually it would be true. 'When should we have this conversation?'

'I'll let you know,' she said, and looked away.

Averting her face intrigued him. What didn't she want him to see in her expression?

'At the moment—' her eyes met his as she resumed the conversation as if whatever had bothered her had been mastered '—I'm confused why an obstetrician would take a job at a tiny maternity unit that deals with healthy low risk women.'

'A valid question.'

'Which I note you haven't answered yet.' She tilted her delightful chin at him and smiled with professional courtesy. 'Why are you here, Ben?'

'You're prickly,' he said conversationally. She wasn't as calm as she made out and that made him feel a little better. 'I think we should talk about that later as well.'

The sound of a vehicle and the rattle of gravel outside heralded a new client and Misty looked away with what he considered disproportionate relief. 'In that case, I've work to do,' she said.

'Work?' She wanted him gone. Well, he wasn't quite ready. 'Sounds interesting, after what you told me at the beach house. Could I see how it pans out? Then I'll slip away.'

'I thought you were done with obstetrics?'

So had he. 'I kept up with the necessary updates and registration.' Funny that. When she didn't answer, Ben prompted her. 'I'll check out the admission CTG. See what the trace's like.' He drifted to the nurses' station and picked up a file as if to check for something.

Misty looked at him strangely then shook her head. There was no doubt he'd exasperated her again. Now what had he said?

'We don't have a foetal monitor here, Ben.'

'What do you mean? Not even external monitors?'

'It's a low-risk unit, remember,' she said. 'We only have low-risk women. Using a machine to electronically listen to a baby that we can hear very well other ways,' she shrugged 'well, that's crazy. Our clinical skills give us all the information we need to know.'

'But the CTG machine allows the baby's heart rate to be recorded on paper at the same time as the mother's contractions. A great indication of the fetal response to the stress of labour.' How could they not want that?

Every hospital he'd ever worked in had used them at least once in every labour. Admittedly they'd all been teaching hospitals, but still.

'Isn't electronic fetal monitoring a part of the protocol of every birth here?' He'd assumed Lyrebird Lake would have a machine somewhere, in a cupboard at least. He'd never heard of a place delivering babies without one.

He breathed deeply.

He supposed the trace didn't guarantee anything, and even when you could hold the results in your hand it didn't mean all was going to go well.

And sometimes well babies showed as unwell babies and intervention that could have been avoided had been performed. Everyone knew that but still, it was the best they had that would stand up in court.

'Not even an admission trace?' He hoped she didn't hear the unhappy note in his voice. This place had to be good for his non-interventionist soul.

'Especially an admission trace. Don't have one, don't want one. We'll talk about this another time. At length.'

He couldn't imagine obstetrics without electronic

screening tools for risk. 'What if you hear the baby's heart rate slow down after a contraction while you're listening?'

'CHICKEN,' she said.

Ben blinked. She hadn't just called him a chicken?

He felt as if he'd been slapped.

Was she an unsafe practitioner? Had he discovered Misty's feet of clay? His stomach plummeted. Surely not? His daughter couldn't birth here and he couldn't work in that environment. He'd made a terrible mistake. He stepped further away from her but she went on.

Rolled her eyes. 'It's an emergency mnemonic, Ben. "C.H." stands for Change Her position. "I" stands for put an IV cannula in and Infuse or Increase her fluid load.

"KE" stands for KEep listening after every contraction. "N" stands for Notify the next level expert...' Her voice trailed off.

Ben's head was spinning. C.H.I.C.K.E.N? He blinked. Ridiculously relieved and then mildly amused. This was the kind of woman he'd sensed Misty would be. Professional and brave enough to stand up to him – and she was also a bit quirky.

CHAPTER 11

Misty

Misty sighed. She'd seen Ben's horror when she'd given him the mnemonic. For her it had been a reflex answer from their emergency practices.

He'd actually thought she'd dared him to play roulette with other people's lives.

That hurt.

If she had more time she'd have been angry but later she would mull it over.

He'd been so quick to damn her practice ethics? Why? Did he honestly think looking after women at one of the most important times in their lives was a thrill ride?

She shook her head to rid herself of the thoughts. Later. She'd sort him out but she didn't have time now. The outside door opened. 'I usually ring the nurse, but you can stay if you want, seeing as your paperwork came through.'

She tried to put him at the back of her mind, knew she couldn't ignore him altogether as she went forward to greet the woman and her anxious partner.

'You're Montana's friend?' the man said and when Misty nodded, he sighed with relief.

'Cherry's waters have broken and she's been wanting to push for the last five minutes in the car. I was that scared she'd pop it out on my seat covers.'

That would be Cherry Glover, Misty thought to herself as she mentally reviewed those 'at term' ladies the unit expected. 'Looks like you made it just in time, then. You must be Ritchie.'

'That's me.'

She turned to the woman. 'Hello, Cherry. We'll have you all set in no time. Come through this way.' She paused at the desk and scooped up Cherry's file. 'This is Dr Moore. He's our new locum and will be staying as the second person because I don't have a nurse at the moment.'

Ben waved and smiled, acknowledging his recruitment, even as Misty moved on to focus on the job at hand. She'd only read Cherry's notes that morning and her case was as uncomplicated as all the women booked to the unit. No risk factors, healthy-sized baby, no blood-pressure problems prior to labour and this was her third healthy pregnancy.

Ritchie was probably right. It was quite on the cards that Cherry was ready to 'pop' this one out. She smiled to herself as Cherry's next contraction was accompanied by a few grunty breaths on Cherry's part. No need to check if she was ready.

Ben assessed the neonatal emergency trolley, a useful thing for him to do, while Misty helped Cherry climb awkwardly out of her damp clothes and wrapped her in a sarong. When her next contraction eased, Misty asked if she was up to climbing onto the bed for a quick abdominal examination and so Misty could listen to the baby's heartbeat.

'Just to check baby's lie. We can use the doppler with you standing after that.'

'No problem, as long as you're quick,' Cherry said, and Misty caught Ben stiffen out of the comer of her eye.

Now, what was up with him?

When Cherry lay down Misty quickly palpated the woman's shiny round abdomen and easily identified the foetal back and the descent of the foetal head into the pelvis.

Everything was great. 'OK, your baby's head is down and engaged nicely. He or she is facing the right way and I'll just have a quick listen.'

Misty counted for a minute with the Pinard's stethoscope, the old-fashioned wooden ear instrument instead of the doppler, and as she turned her ear to Cherry's abdomen, she found herself facing Ben. The expression on his face, though quickly hidden, had shown disbelief and even a tinge of sardonic amusement at her archaic instrument.

'We use this first,' she said to Cherry, but really to Mr Modern Age in the corner, 'to confirm baby's position by the baby's heart rate. It differentiates the mother's pulse so much better than electronics for that first isolation.

Sometimes the electronic equipment can hear the baby all over the place.'

Sound principles, Ben, so get used to it! She hoped her eyes conveyed the message.

He inclined his head so at least he was receptive to her rebuke, she thought grimly, and she straightened and concentrated on her client.

Once she'd confirmed the baby's lie to her satisfaction, she placed the hand-held doppler on Cherry's stomach low down near her pubic bone so the parents could hear the clop, clop, clop of the baby's heartbeat as it filled the room.

Ritchie smiled with relief and Misty grinned, too. 'Your little passenger is very happy in there, even though you've pulled the plug on them.'

She helped Cherry stand up again and smiled at Cherry's sigh from the awkwardness of lying down during the serious end of labour. Even Ben should be able to see how much easier it was for Cherry in an upright position.

'Do you want to lean on the bed?' she asked.

At Cherry's nod, Misty raised the level of the bed so that Cherry could stand and lean against it without bending too much. Misty gently ushered Ritchie behind his wife to massage her lower back in firm circular motions while Cherry breathed through the contraction.

When he was at his task, Misty turned to her own responsibilities. She connected the overhead heater and completed her own check of the baby's emergency trolley then readied her basic equipment for the birth. Quickly took the rest of Cherry's observations: blood pressure, pulse, temperature, and general assessment.

She was still aware of Ben as he leaned against the rear wall of the room, quietly watching.

Concentrate, she chided herself as she began to mentally list her other tasks. All she needed was two clamps for the cord and scissors for Ritchie to cut between the clamps, a dish to catch the placenta and a warm towel and blanket for baby.

No drugs to hasten the placenta, she remembered. 'You've declined the injection after the birth, Cherry. Is that right?'

Cherry gasped as the next pain started. 'I don't want it unless I have to.'

'Have you explained the rationale for oxytocin, Sister?' Ben asked quietly.

Misty froze and then glanced quickly at Cherry and Ritchie, but they didn't seem to have heard as the woman's breathing increased in tempo.

'We discuss it at antenatal visits, yes,' Misty said, and then added, 'A woman's choice.'

Then she ignored him and ran warm water into a bowl before she slipped her gloves on to dip a washcloth into the warm fluid and wait. No time to run the bath.

Cherry moaned and Ritchie yelped as a small trickle of blood ran down his wife's leg. 'She's haemorrhaging,' he gasped, and Misty smiled.

'That's a sign of labour. It's okay, Ritchie. That "shows" Cherry's cervix, or the opening at the bottom of the uterus, is opening and her time is near. She's showing all the signs of not long now. After she's had the baby, I'll get you to put the electric bed down to low level again so Cherry can lie back.'

'You mean she's having it standing up?' Ritchie cast a

horrified look in Misty's direction before his wife recalled his attention.

'That's what she asked for.'

'Fabulous,' Ben whispered with the tiniest hint of sarcasm, and Misty frowned. One more negative comment and she'd ask him to leave.

'Keep rubbing!' Cherry's command was almost a growl and Misty bit her lip to stop her smile again. Cherry was running this show, not Ben Moore.

'If Cherry didn't want to be in this position,' she said to Ritchie, and without looking at him, to Ben, 'she'd move. Everything is fine. Now, do you see the controls for the bed, there, Ritchie?' Misty pointed. 'I'll tell you when to move it back down.'

Ritchie gulped at that much responsibility and Cherry moaned loudly.

Misty slipped in next to Ritchie. She placed her warm towel for the baby on the bed beside her client.

'OK, Cherry,' she said. 'Nice and easy. I'm just going to put my hand down here with a warm washcloth to help that burning feeling as baby's head comes through.'

She felt the baby's occiput bulge under her hand as Cherry pushed, and suddenly the head was out.

'Whoops. That was quick.' Misty smiled. 'That's great, Cherry, your baby's head's born. Take some little breaths if the pain has gone or push again if you need to.'

'Oh, my God,' Ritchie muttered distantly as his knees wobbled and he swayed limply against Misty as his legs gave way.

'Just sit for a minute, mate.' Ben's calm voice came from behind Misty's shoulder as he nudged Ritchie into the chair he'd pushed in beside the bed. The new father collapsed. Ben firmly placed Ritchie's head between his knees and bounced him twice. 'Take a few breaths, mate.'

At least Ben could do something constructive. That was a relief. Misty grinned without turning as she kept one hand on the baby's head. She flicked open the warm towel and rested it on the little scalp as she waited.

Cherry pushed again and baby rotated until a shoulder appeared, then the rest of baby unfolded into Misty's towel-wrapped hands in a flurry of limbs. Misty slipped the baby, still joined by the umbilical cord, through Cherry's legs to Ben who had appeared usefully in the perfect position. He gently wiped the little body before passing her naked baby up to Cherry.

Cherry dropped her sarong unselfconsciously to bare her skin for baby, who mewled like a little kitten and then settled when she was snuggled against her mother's warm skin.

'What is it?' Ritchie's voice was muffled from his position but cracked with emotion. Misty and Ben waited quietly for Cherry to look.

'It's my girl,' Cherry sobbed as she hugged the squirming baby to her chest. 'Hello, Phoebe. Hello my darling little girl.'

'Just push that button and lower the bed so Cherry can sit down, Ritchie.' She glanced at the new father but he'd returned his head between his knees.

'I've got it,' Ben murmured from behind her left ear, and the whirr of the bed mechanism underlined his presence. Suddenly she was glad he was there, so his sceptical self would see that everything was normal.

He'd even been a little handy.

Cherry eased onto the bed with her baby against her

chest and Ben draped a blanket over both of them. After a few minutes Misty lifted the edge of the blanket and offered Ritchie the scissors. 'Are you going to cut the cord, Ritchie?'

'Can't.' Ritchie's voice was muffled from his hands over his face. 'Maybe in a minute.'

'No rush.' Misty tucked the blanket back as they waited.

After a further few minutes Ritchie reached across and Misty showed him where to cut. 'I need to push again.' Cherry knew what came next as the placenta was delivered into the dish Misty held.

Misty held up the bowl. 'Did you want to see this, Cherry? These are incredible things. I always think of placentas as amazing little heart-lung machines that incubate babies beautifully.'

'I've never looked before,' Cherry said, and she craned her neck curiously when Misty held up the thin membranous bag.

'This is where baby lived inside you,' Misty expanded the membrane so the pale balloon shaped bag hung as if baby was still inside. 'The shiny side is inside the bag and you can see the place where the umbilical cord is connected.'

'Wow. Check this out, Ritchie.' Cherry was impressed but Ritchie kept his head averted now he'd lifted it enough to see his daughter.

'No way,' he replied with a visible shudder. 'I'd much rather look at Phoebe.'

Misty smiled at Cherry and took the placenta away.

Ritchie stroked his baby's cheek and smiled tearily at Cherry. 'She's like you, honey. Gorgeous.' And he stood up carefully and leaned over and kissed his wife. Looked at Ben. 'Women are freakin' incredible.'

He shook his head in disbelief that it was all over and his daughter was safely in front of him.

Misty tucked the warmed blanket around Cherry's shoulders after ensuring her uterus had started contracting to control bleeding. She quickly checked Cherry's blood pressure and pulse again while Ben listened to Phoebe's lungs, thankfully without disturbing her, as she nudged at her mother's breast.

'We'll leave you three to get acquainted,' Misty said quietly. 'I'll be back in five minutes and I'm just outside if you need anything.'

The new parents nodded as Misty and Ben left the room and the door shut quietly behind them.

CHAPTER 12

Ben

'At the lake we don't appreciate disruptive comments in the birthing suite, Ben.'

Misty glared at him and Ben blinked because he hadn't seen it coming. Green sparks burned holes in his forehead as he took a step back. He didn't understand how he could have missed her displeasure in the room.

'Did I do that?' He hadn't intended to be negative. Couldn't recall what he'd said to inspire such a full-blooded rebuke. 'Would you care to elaborate?'

'There were a few sceptical comments I could have done without,' she said quietly. 'I'm hoping Cherry didn't hear them.'

Misty put the chart down as if it were made of cracked fragile crystal. So carefully, he had the impression she wanted to slam it through the desk. Amazing how much more powerful her restraint was. The woman was never boring.

'I apologise.' He thought back over the time since he'd arrived. He may have muttered something about the patient standing up. It wasn't something he would choose as an optimum position for the person actually catching the baby. 'Did she choose upright or did you?'

Misty compressed her lips, which only served to draw attention to something he was trying not to think about, her gorgeously unpredictable mouth. Consciously he cut the thought off.

Misty closed her eyes as if exasperated with him. 'Did you have your ears shut when she sighed with relief at getting off the bed?'

He thought back to that. Maybe he had heard that. But he was more interested in the post birth injection. 'Antenatally, do you not encourage injections after the birth?' He raised his eyebrows sceptically. 'Or do all the women mystically come to the same conclusion and decline off their own bat?'

She smiled sweetly but there was steel beneath the surface. 'They choose, Ben. That's what this place is all about. Choice. You'll have to get used to it or this isn't the place for you.' Glanced at her watch. 'Five minutes. I need to go and repeat my post birth observations on the mother and baby. I'd prefer you stayed here.'

So he stayed and she went.

He thought about the last fifteen or so minutes. She meant everything she said. She really did. He thought about the conversation, about what he'd just witnessed and what he knew about Misty, the woman who had saved his life and calmly driven away.

And the baby's outcome? Perfect. Peaceful. Calm. Happy parents.

By the time he'd thought it all through she was back, for another five minutes he presumed. She had twin spots of colour in her cheeks.

'I'm sorry if I was rude,' she said calmly.

'You weren't rude.'

'I was disappointed.' As if she didn't hear him. 'That's all.'

In him. Disappointed in him. It stung.

He could almost understand why, but if he did manage not to get thrown out of here he guessed he'd understand better very soon. 'Well, the birth was incredible. Thank you for allowing me to stay.'

'You're welcome.' It sounded like an automatic response, without emotion.

He really was glad of the opportunity to get an early impression of how they did things here. How much his work could evolve into something different. Perhaps he'd even find some of the passion he used to have for birth before machines medicalised passion out of existence. 'I guess it's such a different style from my last hospital. It will take me a few days to get used to it.'

Now she looked nonplussed. 'Are you saying you've forgotten how natural birth can be? That doesn't make sense when I know you must have seen hundreds of babies enter the world.'

'I'm the bloke they called in when disaster hit. Or women and babies were high risk. When the machines you hate so much are desperately needed. Different spectrum of labour and birth.'

Her set face relaxed a little as she smiled. 'I was

surprised at your comments during the birth, but coming from that setting perhaps I see where they come from. You were helpful at the end.'

'Thank you.' He withheld his own smile, pleased she'd given him a little benefit of the doubt. 'It's a mental swing from being the primary obstetrician to a midwife's helper here.'

'Cherry was amazing,' she said as if she wanted to lighten the atmosphere. 'Thanks for steering Ritchie into the chair. It's always distracting when the dad faints beside me.'

'The least I could do.' His thoughts were elsewhere.

The more he thought about it the more Ben's mind grappled with something he seemed to have lost sight of years ago. The joy of birth. It had, actually, been far too long since he'd seen a normal birth. Seen a healthy woman and no interference from the birth attendant. But the element of risk he was tuned to, even if it was imagined or ingrained, meant leaving everything to nature would take some getting used to.

A flicker of familiar unease and the darkness he'd like to have left behind caught up with him. They were still playing with life here and he'd seen what bad outcomes could do to people. 'I'm not happy about the lack of injection after the birth.'

Misty looked up at him as if he'd just blasphemed and he found his mouth twitching at what was becoming a standard response from her.

'The medication is there if we need it. And we would use it.' The edge was back in her voice and he realised he'd ignited her zeal more than he'd intended. 'But we seldom do. Doesn't that fact make you think of all those women who have interference that isn't warranted?'

He shook his head. 'No. It makes me think of the controlled randomised studies that prove oxytocin after the birth of the baby decreases the risk of postpartum haemorrhage in hospitals.'

Misty nodded but there was a glint in her eye. 'I think the key word is "hospitals". Why do you think women have more haemorrhages in hospital, Ben?' She tapped a finger against the corner of her mouth. 'Hmmm. I wonder.'

She was daring him to get into a technical discussion with her. No problem, lady, he thought, and mentally rubbed his hands. 'Enlighten me.'

She raised her finely arched brows, not one whit intimidated by his confidence of winning a medical debate. 'I've already said it. Interference,' she said. 'That's why.'

'Isn't this a hospital?'

'No, it's a birth centre. Women-centred care for healthy pregnant women. Who birth here and go home.' She looked at her watch. 'To be continued. Another five minutes is up. I'll be back.'

While she was gone he thought about her response and conceded that the more qualifications and experience he had, the more the system seemed to thrust him into intervention and diagnostics. Statistics from complicated labours might not be as valid here, but they were valid where he'd come from.

Then again, he hadn't been anywhere like this place in all his time as a doctor. Misty seemed perfectly at home here. This place was amazing but he wasn't going to tell her that.

He'd like to see their records of birth. Numbers. Outcomes. Staffing. How it all worked. A lot of things he usually wasn't curious about and it wasn't all due to his particular interest in Misty. Though she was a part of it.

How much specialist antenatal care did women really receive here? Were there improvements he could make? Did he have something to offer these practitioners who seemed to have it all under control?

Misty came back. Walked past him to the desk and sat down at the computer. She opened a file and ticked some boxes before she began typing.

'Did Cherry even have an ultrasound during pregnancy?'

She looked up at him. 'Andy likes the clients booked here to have one ultrasound at least.' Misty's brows drew together and from the frown he guessed she didn't think all the women needed that either. That amused him. 'They have scans at eighteen weeks into the pregnancy. Other than that we answer ultrasound questions with good antenatal care and hands-on assessment.'

There was challenge in the last words. He'd seen her hands on. Impressive. 'As it should be,' he said. He'd bet the midwives here had top-notch clinical skills with all that hands-on experience. 'So how does this place work with staff?'

She grinned at that as if the mention of staff made her smile. Misty was jotting times and names in the birth register and had recovered her good humour. He should take a leaf out of her book and learn to get over things once they were discussed.

Maybe he wouldn't have turned into the person he was.

'I call a second person in for the birth.' She answered absently, her attention back on the computer screen. 'In case they need to go for something or call for help, but otherwise they're only an observer. You have to remember these are low-risk women doing what they are designed to do.'

'Low risk is still risk.' Spoken like a doctor, he thought, but that was what he was.

Misty paused. Looked at him. 'Women feel more confident if they know they will be free of unnecessary interference. Like Montana. A woman who proved she can birth on her own if she had no choice.'

All his misgivings came back. He couldn't banish the spectre of worrying if something went wrong. The spectre of the past. 'So you look after them on your own or with another midwife?'

Misty must have picked up on his unease because a firmer note entered her voice and she turned to give him her undivided attention. Her scrutiny drilling into him. 'Or a nurse, or Andy if no one else is around. Now, I guess, you.'

All he could think of were the hordes of people available in the hospital he'd worked at. Midwives, nurses, registrars, paediatricians, all on call or a few minutes away. And still they'd had their tragedies. With terrible ramifications.

'What if everyone is busy and can't get away? What if two women come in at once?'

Misty shrugged. Obviously she had no such qualms. 'Then I manage with the woman's support person and phone for help if I need it. Didn't Andy explain the unit to you?'

No, and I'm far from comfortable, Ben thought, but he didn't say it because he'd only just got here. And somehow he was still on the back foot with Misty. He hadn't figured how or why that had happened yet, but she had a habit of throwing him off kilter.

So instead he said, 'Andy hasn't really had the time. He said he'd deal with any problems but apparently problems are rare.'

Ben heard the words coming out of his mouth. Dribble and he knew it. He was a doctor. And a man. It was his job to fix things and the concept that nothing would require his particular skills was an interesting one to grapple with.

Misty was more than comfortable, he could see that, and he realised suddenly that he envied her. She'd found her place to make her difference. She was at home here. Perfectly in control.

'Problems are rare,' she said, 'because with well women and well babies and with good, observant hands-on care, birth is a natural event, not an illness. We handle trouble efficiently if it happens, and then we refer on to specialist centres. This is woman-centred care, so guess who the most important person is?'

He could hear the challenge in her voice and he didn't like the inference she expected him to disagree. Despite the fact he'd just pondered it himself. 'Why would you think I would have a problem with the woman being the most important person in the room?'

'It's been my experience with some obstetricians. Some like to ask for as many machines as possible to record variables inside the woman, but not ask the woman. They think the more equipment required the better.' She looked up at him and raised her eyebrows. 'Are you one of those?'

He shrugged, unwilling to get into another argument. Misty had no such qualms. He could tell she was fiercely protective about the way they worked at the lake.

'To a real birth attendant,' she continued, 'a woman shows in her behaviour how her labour is progressing. The fact you've spent time with that woman helps the attendant pick up subtle changes too.'

Ben frowned. 'Not all the time. We've all seen quiet achievers, and I think that even a generalised statement about "some" obstetricians is unfair.' He added quietly.

She ran a hand over her eyes. 'You're right,' she said. 'It was a generalisation. I apologise. I guess I'm still a little shocked to see you.'

Of course, she was more tense than usual because he was there. And how typical of her not to have an issue apologising. He could take a leaf out of her book.

In retrospect he should have at least warned her he was coming, now that he thought about it. And he hadn't even mentioned he'd brought his pregnant daughter who he wanted her to care for.

'I'm sorry. I should have contacted you.' But what would he have done if she, had said don't come?

'Thank you.' She swung away from him. 'Now I do have work to do.'

'I'll help,' he said, and she paused as if she was going to say something then changed her mind. 'Fine,' was all she said, so he followed her while she cleaned her trolley and washed instruments.

She had the delightful stride of a woman on a mission and he could have watched her all day. Gloves were donned as she checked the placenta to ensure all of the lobes were present and accounted for, and he realised he'd forgotten that someone else ensured all this happened behind the scenes, because a missing lobe of placenta could indicate a

high risk of bleeding for the woman. The carer needed to know.

He watched her examine the cross-section of umbilical cord to check there were two arteries and a vein. If only one artery instead of the usual two was present then the baby had an increased risk of kidney problems.

This was like a refresher at uni, only his current lecturer looked nothing like the professor he'd had for anatomy.

Misty went back into the birth room and stripped the bed, and he helped her. Not something he usually did for the midwife, but Misty didn't seem to think it was a strange thing for him to do.

Ben looked around. These were all new experiences and he was actually enjoying himself. 'Where's our new baby?'

Misty looked across the room at the closed bathroom door and smiled at Ben's use of the possessive adjective. 'In the shower with Mum and Dad. I've just done the observations.'

Ben blinked. 'All three of them?'

'It's a big shower with two water roses.' Misty grinned at the disbelief in his voice and he tried to sound less stressed.

He told himself that if he'd arrived this afternoon

instead of when he had, then nothing would be different, except that he wouldn't have known how laid back it was here.

That didn't stop his brain from chanting about infant hypoglycaemia from thermal stress.

'Won't the baby get cold?' He thought he sounded quite upbeat considering the worried state of his mind.

'Of course she won't.' She didn't quite say he was looking for trouble but the inference came through in her tone. 'Where were you when skin-to-skin contact for the first hour of life came in? She'll be warmer against their skin than wrapped up in blankets, that's for sure.'

As if she needed to prove this to him, she strode to the bathroom and knocked on the door. 'You all still okay in there?'

'Yep.' Ritchie sounded confident, finally. 'Did you want us to come out?'

'Only when you're ready. I'll go and make us all a cup of tea and some toast for five minutes.'

Ben sighed. Maybe it was just him. 'I've been out of obstetrics for too long.'

Even that admission didn't win him any points. 'Ha,' she said, as if all her suspicions had been proven correct. 'That's what I mean. This isn't obstetrics. This is normal birth. Later this year we're hoping to extend to births at home for those who choose that, with our midwives of course.'

No way. Ben blinked. He'd never be involved in home births. 'That won't happen in a hospital system.'

She put her hands on her hips, and it reminded him of the day they'd first met. The day she'd scolded him for being so flippant about his life. Suddenly his concerns about the running of this unit dissipated. She had the bit between her teeth and he doubted he could stop her even if he wanted to.

Strange how differently this woman affected him compared with anyone he'd known before. How she made him adjust his thinking, add shades of grey he'd never have considered because he valued her body and mind and emotions as a whole. Even from their brief acquaintance, he knew on some deep inner level that Misty would change his life forever, even if only by passing through it.

He secretly hoped she'd have a great effect on his daughter, too. Maybe she'd have them both fully educated before the end of Tammy's pregnancy.

'Wrong,' she said, and he couldn't remember what now he was 'wrong' about. Actually, right this minute with her standing in front of him, fire in her eyes and hands on her hips, everything seemed rosily right. Also, he wanted to kiss her.

'Home birth already happens in a dozen health services that I know of. Montana and I have a friend, Mia, coming from Coffs Harbour to run that side of it.'

He nodded because he'd better look like he was listening when all he could think about was how wonderful she'd tasted the last time they'd kissed. Totally inappropriate, given the work environment and her general disapproval of him.

'And why not?' she added. 'Statistics prove the less intervention the better the outcome. Home birth is the norm in many countries.'

Ben rubbed his forehead. He was not getting into this discussion. It would be best if he took his libido for a walk and came back later. 'I'd better go and see my boss. Andy said he'd meet me over at administration if I arrived early.'

Misty stopped and looked at him. 'Oh. Okay.' She even looked slightly shamefaced at her fervour. What if she'd been just as off balance as he was at their meeting again? He felt like slapping himself on the forehead. Of course she was. She'd told him so earlier.

'I think what you do here is amazing, Misty. I'm sorry I didn't get it more quickly.'

He needed to clarify the real reason he was there, that being Tammy. Maybe they both needed discussion but not now. Not when he had the urge to pull her into his arms and she had no such urge.

'I'll be back later,' he said, but couldn't resist turning back one last time. 'It's really good to see you again, Misty.'

Then he forced himself to walk away. Ben didn't know what he'd expected when he'd come to Lyrebird Lake. He'd thought more about Tammy's situation and seeing if the connection was still there with Misty, in that order, rather than work, but he'd always assumed he'd manage the work side.

But this was more than a little different to his previous positions; this was way outside his comfort zone.

Andy told him the hospital was busier now than it had been as more families moved into the lake area from the mine. Andy said he'd spend most of his days seeing outpatients, ensuring the inpatients continued to improve, and be back-up for Maternity if any patients needed transfer to the base hospital. No expectation of him being there for births.

Surprisingly, he had the feeling he was going to love

the extra dimensions of the general practice nature of the job.

And unsurprisingly, despite the unusual first meeting this morning, the connection with Misty was still there, on his side anyway. But he needed to push that back to where it belonged in his priority list. He was there for Tammy, not to explore a relationship with Misty—not that she was likely to have him anyway.

He was far too much the obstetrician to appeal to a woman like her. That was fine.

Misty had been right in rejecting him at the beach. Her life held merit and direction and she didn't need him and his problems on a personal level.

Something else tugged at him. Niggled with concern. This morning, in that first appraisal in the empty wing before the patient arrived, when Misty had looked up with such anxiety and even a flicker of fear at the prospect of an intruder. He'd have a talk to Andy about safeguards in case some crazy did go to Maternity looking for drugs or money.

Misty, and the other women of course, needed to be safe in their workplace.

He found himself whistling. Something he hadn't done in years. Despite the rollercoaster of Misty, and the learning curve of the women-centred-care, suddenly he felt a surge of optimism and purpose.

He'd needed somewhere secure to take his stepdaughter, while she was still reeling from the implications of her pregnancy. Hopefully Tammy would agree with his first impression. Lyrebird Lake felt right.

Perhaps it was the place that could help heal them both.

CHAPTER 13

Misty

Misty kept thinking about Ben. There was so much unsaid between them she didn't know where to start, and she'd been spouting her passion for how great they were here because she'd wanted to fill the silences.

But she could have done with a few answers herself. Like where he was living and when she could expect to see him next so she could prepare herself.

'It's nice to see you, too, Ben,' she murmured, but of course he didn't hear because he was long gone.

She'd bombarded him with zealous comments about the unit. Driving him away intentionally?

She thought about that explanation and maybe it was true because she really hadn't come to terms with his effect on her. Especially this new, polished and professional, once she'd nudged him, Ben. Today had at least confirmed for her that the impact from the first meeting hadn't only been about the adrenalin rush of life/death situation.

By late that afternoon Cherry, Ritchie and baby Phoebe had packed up and returned home and the maternity unit was shut again.

Misty walked across the park and up the drive to the big old doctors' house that catered for visiting staff to the hospital. She'd moved in there when she started work, never having intended to stay with Montana and Andy and their little family, and she loved the relaxed feel of the old house.

The residence was run by Louisa, a round Yorkshire dumpling of a woman with merry eyes and big breasts, who'd hugged and kissed Misty's cheek at their initial meeting and loved to spoil her. Apparently she'd spoiled Montana and her baby, Dawn, with equal fervour when they'd lived there.

Ned, the other resident, while supposedly semiretired as a GP, was a busy little Scotsman who ran a clinic every afternoon in a rundown set of consulting rooms at the end of the house. He hobbled a little with his stiff hip, and he and Louisa were an 'item.'

'Good afternoon, Ned.' Misty smiled at the elderly gentleman as she arrived home.

Ned sat on the veranda that faced the hospital and carved a fat wombat out of driftwood with more gusto than artistry. 'Hello there, Misty. So we've another change to the house.'

Misty's stomach took a dive. She'd almost convinced herself Ben would stay at the upmarket guest house on the lake but, of course, he was staying here! Murphy's law. She plastered a smile on her face. 'Dr Moore. Yes, I've met him.'

'He says you've more than met him,' Ned said archly, and Misty felt her face flame. Surely not.

'You're blushing, missy.' Ned chuckled. 'No need to be embarrassed about saving someone's life.'

Misty only just stopped herself from saying, *Oh, that.* Instead, she looked away at the distant hospital and said, 'I don't like to think about it, that's all.'

'Fair enough.' Ned nodded sagely. 'So we've a couple of new boarders.'

'A couple?' Misty stopped as she reached for the screen door handle.

'The new doctor and his daughter. Didn't you know about her? About sixteen, lots of attitude and pregnant with it.' He sighed heavily as he returned to his carving. 'Reminds me of my son when he was a teen and his girl-friend was pregnant.'

'You have a son?' Her voice came out wooden but she was trying to focus on Ned's unexpected sharing. Instead of the shock of Ben and his unknown daughter.

'Indeed. We fell out when he went into the army.'

'I'm sorry to hear you fell out, Ned. I hope he contacts you soon.' She smiled at him. 'And I'm surprised to hear Ben has a daughter.' A pregnant daughter. Here was a whole world she knew nothing about. The teenage daughter of the man whose life she'd saved and whose arms she'd slept in.

Did that mean Ben wasn't here to see her at all? That

she'd been all hot under the collar for nothing. That he was here for the birth-centre she'd told him all about?

Cold disappointment settled on her stomach.

That put a whole new slant on things and, really, it gave her the excuse she'd needed to shut down that attraction she'd been fighting this morning. She thought about it some more. So, despite the fact he'd infuriated her with his closed mind about procedures in the birth centre, he'd actually come to take advantage of it.

Perhaps knowing this made more sense. His questioning. Because he had a special reason to worry. He would want what's best for his daughter.

How was she going to face Ben's daughter, possibly as a patient, when she had problems facing Ben? She opened the door. With her chin up, she guessed. That was all she could do.

Ben's entry into her life had certainly provided a whole host of new situations to be challenged with but life was a challenge. Lucky she'd kept her professional shield up or she'd be cringing that she'd assumed he'd felt the same attraction she had. Phew.

She squeezed her eyes shut and then opened one to peer at Ned. 'Are they both here now?'

'Aye.' Ned nodded sagely as he whittled at his wombat's legs. 'The wee one is in the kitchen with Louisa and Ben.'

The 'wee one' was almost six feet tall and towered over Misty when she went in to meet her.

Misty didn't look at Ben. She couldn't.

'Ah, here's Misty,' Louisa said placidly. 'This is Tammy, Dr Moore's daughter, and you've met Ben, I hear.'

The first thing about Tammy, apart from her height,

was her magnificent blue eyes, just like Ben's. She needed to stop thinking about Ben's eyes. Truly, she did...

She concentrated on the daughter she hadn't known existed but her mouth followed her brain, unfortunately. 'Hello there, Tammy. You have your father's eyes.'

The girl tugged at the hem of a bulky sweater, unusual in the Queensland heat and obviously worn to disguise her pregnancy. She sniffed. 'He's not my real father, just my stepfather.'

'Tammy!' Ben admonished, and Misty opened and shut her mouth unable to think of anything to say.

Dear, sweet, unflappable Louisa had the situation under control. 'Smooth your feathers, young woman,' she said calmly. 'Misty is the person you'll be needing in a while when that babe of yours comes along.'

Misty smiled at Louisa for steering the situation back onto even ground. Then she turned the same bright smile to Tammy. 'You'll be fine. Welcome anyway, Tammy. I hope you'll settle in easily here.'

She glanced at Ben, who was clearly unhappy with his "daughter", and she began to wonder at their relationship before she stopped herself. It was all too complicated and none of her business. Instead, she stepped across to hug Louisa. 'And how are you?'

Louisa patted her arm. 'I'm fine. You know I love guests. The more the merrier. Now, you scoot along and get changed and Tammy can set the table while you're gone. Ben will pour a glass of wine for you on the back veranda.'

Louisa knew how to organise people. That was one of the first things Misty had discovered when she'd moved into the residence and one of the most endearing. She scooted, as instructed, and while she showered and changed she remembered the look of hurt on Ben's face at Tammy's disclosure.

More things she didn't understand about Ben.

Tammy was Ben's stepdaughter. So, who had been looking after her while Ben had lived at his beach house? There'd been no sign and certainly no mention of anyone else living there. Except for those shells glued to the bathroom mirror, she remembered suddenly, and possibly the constellations on the bedroom ceiling.

It had been hard to discern just how pregnant Tammy was, between the voluminous sweater and the girl's slouchy posture, so that gave no clues on how long they would be staying.

But there was no doubt in Misty's mind that Tammy's pregnancy was the real reason for Ben coming there. How she felt about this would take a lot of thinking through. But where was the girl's mother?

LATER THAT AFTERNOON, when the sun was setting behind the lake, Misty stepped out onto the veranda. She'd grown to love the view across the water. The trees around the shore reflected in the stillness of the water so they looked twice as tall and strong and imposing. Tiny canoes and kayaks zigzagged across the water, disturbing flocks of waterbirds.

Every afternoon at sunset a new array of colours transformed the sky.

Ben was seated on the swing chair, swaying back and forwards as if unable to keep still, and he stood up as she closed the door behind her.

The lake faded into the distance and suddenly all she could see was him. Big, dark, brooding. And not here at Lyrebird Lake for her at all.

His gaze drifted appreciatively over her T-shirt and jeans and something she'd randomly chosen was suddenly a satisfying choice. Funny how an attractive man could make you feel that way just by looking at you, she thought wryly.

Ben leant on the rail. Shoulders and feet wide. Magnetically male in front of her. Drawing her in with his presence. It was hard to remember this was the same man she'd dragged unconscious onto her lost boogie board. The thought gave her pause.

He waved her over. 'Here. Have this seat. The view's very pleasant from here,' he said, but the glint in his eye suggested he wasn't talking about the lake, and she felt that warmth of pleasure again. She really had to stop reacting so effusively to him. It wouldn't do.

'Thank you.' Against her better judgement, she sat down. It would have been churlish to refuse, but she unobtrusively crossed her fingers that he wouldn't end up hip to hip with her because she didn't think she could cope with that much proximity. She knew where proximity to Ben could lead. 'The lake is pretty, isn't it?'

Thankfully he didn't sit beside her on the swing, but he was still too close when he pulled a chair up next to her and sat. 'Different from the ocean.'

'True.'

How long could they chat about the view before one of them fell asleep? she mockingly asked herself. Yet she couldn't bring herself to talk of substantial things, not with him so close and her senses skipping with a combination of joy and nerves at this proximity. She looked away from him to the colours in the sky. Was about to say something inane about the sunset when Ben spoke.

'I've thought about you a lot, Misty.'

Her eyes widened. Ah, Ben. There you go, diving right in.

'Have you?' Said airily. *I find that hard to believe. You haven't rung, you obviously figured out where to find me, and it's been a month.* She probably should restrain herself but after the frank discussion in the ward today, she decided he could take truth. She wasn't going to hide when he annoyed her. 'Hard to miss someone if you don't know anything about them.'

'I'd like to think that isn't true.'

If he stretched out his hand, he could have taken her fingers in his. He didn't, but just the thought of that possible contact had her sliding her hand unobtrusively under the back of her leg and out of reach.

Ben saw, grimaced, didn't comment, and went on softly, 'Actually, I think we learnt a lot about each other in a very short time.'

Well, she certainly had some blanks in his past. 'Do you have any more children?' she asked dryly. 'A wife, somewhere?'

As soon as the words left her mouth she regretted them. It really was none of her business. She'd been a stranger, spending brief time with him making sure he didn't die from complications. There'd been nothing else. Just her own odd feelings and sensations of knowing him more than she did.

'There's just Tammy.'

No wife then?

He offered her a top up for her glass of wine which she knew she wouldn't drink. She was having enough trouble keeping control of her mouth without alcohol; the last thing she needed was to blurt out something she'd really regret.

'Thank you,' she said, and rested the glass on the table beside her. Frustratingly, she couldn't stop the shake in her fingers.

Of course he didn't miss it. The way he was looking at her he wouldn't miss anything. 'What's wrong?'

'Nothing.' She looked away and then back at him. 'Though it is a little awkward to be talking to you here.'

He raised his eyebrows. 'Why? I thought we communicated very well this morning and the first time we met.'

She looked away and her voice dropped. 'We didn't communicate, Ben, we kissed. And if I hadn't left when I did we would have slept together in the true sense of the word.'

'But you did leave and still you made a big impact on me. I'm here for Tammy, as you've no doubt worked out. But that's not all. I chose here, Lyrebird Lake, because of you.'

Ignoring the last, suspiciously like an afterthought on his part, concentrating on Tammy, she said brightly, 'So, how long are you staying? It's certainly good timing for Andy and Montana.'

Ben sighed at her change of tack and she frowned a little at her own cowardice. He'd dived right into talk of their attraction, so why couldn't she be honest? Why should she feel embarrassed for something that didn't happen?

To make it worse, he allowed himself to be diverted

and contrarily she didn't want that either. Although he sipped his wine before addressing her questions. 'It's good timing for Tammy, too. Her school has suspended her and her grandmother and Tammy have fallen out over her pregnancy. I've wanted to get Tammy away from both for a while now.'

'Both?'

'The school. Her grandmother's inability to keep her safe. The crowd she's fallen in with.'

'So you hope Lyrebird Lake will be good for your step-daughter?'

'I do. But I should say I refuse to call Tammy my step-daughter because until my wife's death I'd never suspected she wasn't my own.'

His wife's death? Then there really was only him and Tammy.

Misty's voice softened. He'd just revealed big stuff to her. Surprising stuff. Tough gig, Ben. 'That must have been a shock.'

Wow. She could only imagine the impact it had on him.

He went on. 'It took away any chance of my input into her life when she was in her grandmother's care. We never got on. Tammy's grandmother was given custody over her after my wife's death because of that confirmation.'

'That must have been hard.' Really hard, Misty thought.

'First steps, first words, first day at school—you can't erase parenting with a DNA test result. All I can hope is that Tammy does understand that I still love her as my daughter. She's been mine since she was born.'

Ben stood up abruptly, as if he couldn't sit still with so much emotion racing through him. 'Lyrebird Lake could be a great place.'

'It is a great place.'

He turned to face her. 'Andy told me there's another young woman a little older than Tammy, with a two-year-old, who runs a young mums' class. I heard you were involved in that, too.'

'That's right.' He'd done his homework, Misty had to admit. 'Emma is great. I'd be happy to introduce the two girls if they agree. Emma's started uni part time, studying to be a midwife.'

She wondered now what she wanted from this man, who'd shared a big part of his past with her, but still remained a mystery. Sure, they had chemistry but was that worth pursuing? Did they have anything in common besides the tenuous link of how they met?

What was realistic? She guessed that depended.

'How long are you staying, Ben?' This is what she wanted to know. Needed to know. To work out how she was going to approach managing her feelings towards him.

Ben gazed out over the lake. 'I expect to stay at the very least a month, with an option to extend after that. Tammy's baby is due in four weeks.'

A month or more. Her stomach fluttered with the news. How was she going to cope with that?

'Tammy's that close? I could hardly tell she was pregnant.' She sounded like a simpleton but Misty's mind spun with times and dates. She took a sip of the wine because she couldn't possibly get more addlebrained. 'That makes Tammy due the same time as Montana. Goodness.'

'It's not a big baby,' Ben went on, oblivious to Misty's mental squirming. 'She hides her bump in those heavy jumpers no matter what the weather and hasn't been eating well.'

Misty could see the concern etched into his face and in his tense posture. Gratefully she allowed herself to be drawn away from her own worries. 'Queensland's heat will make camouflage a bit trickier. I think the sooner we get her and Emma together the better.'

'I agree. On both counts.'

She thought back to his reactions this morning in the unit. 'How do you feel about having your grandchild born in a birth centre?'

He looked away to the view and she wondered why. He managed to hide what he was thinking much more successfully than she could. 'You said it was the best. That's why we're here.'

'Lyrebird Lake is the best,' she agreed, 'but you haven't answered my question.'

He smiled ruefully. 'How do I feel?' A tight shrug. 'I'm worried.'

Ah. No surprise there. 'About?'

'Mainly... I fear she won't be able to cope with the pain of contractions, not having the option of an epidural or strong drugs. I won't be able to help her once she's in labour in this environment.'

At least he was being honest, Misty acknowledged, but he just didn't get it. It wasn't his fault. It was his training in the big hospital system. 'In that case, she could transfer out. But is she the one that won't cope or is it you, Ben?'

He shrugged, and she could see he wasn't willing to go there. 'It's not just the labour. I'm worried that she'll get sick, worried that she'll get postnatal depression because her mother did, with tragic consequences. Tammy has a risk of that.'

Ben definitely had demons.

'All women have some risk of depression, Ben, and maybe there is more risk for Tammy, but that can be monitored. Watched for after the birth. Physically she's a normal teenager, yes? Younger women than Tammy have been having babies in other cultures since the beginning of time.'

'But not my daughter.' The anguish was real in his voice and she wanted to hug him and tell him Tammy would be fine. Tammy's mother's history of depression was a real concern, of course.

She didn't know what she could say to help him but she would try. 'I'm sure you said you wrote a book on postnatal depression. That makes you an expert, so you should have that covered. Tell me, Ben, are there any good feelings about this pregnancy in your head?'

He frowned. 'Of course there are, or will be, when she's safely delivered.'

Ha! She had him.

Misty raised her brows at Ben. 'She won't be "delivered" if she has her baby here, Ben.' She held his gaze. 'She'll give birth and we'll support her.' Misty couldn't resist rubbing the pedantic in, albeit with a smile and a twinkle in her eye, and reluctantly he smiled back.

'Okay.' He held up his hands in surrender. 'Women-centred care—non-intervention, not "delivery". I can feel the grey hairs already. And that's not counting trying to be a parent to a teenage girl I really do need help with.'

Ahhhhh. Misty leaned back. That was what he wanted

from her. That was it. Why he'd come. To help him, short term, to understand how to parent his teenage daughter and be there when she gave birth.

It wasn't an onerous thought but it stung a little when it came with his stated "connection" to her.

Misty allowed the wispy dreams of Ben being irresistibly attracted to her dissolve into vapour. 'I understand a little of what she's feeling, Ben.'

He looked at her.

'My mother died when I was young and as a teen I was angry. That's when a young woman needs her mother most. And again when she's pregnant. I understand her mother may not be alive, but Tammy has you.'

He nodded.

She dived in. 'And her grandmother, if not both together. She's not alone. Just like I have Andy, and now Montana.'

Ben searched her face as if to see if she really believed what she'd said. 'So you're saying I've done the right thing, bringing her here.'

Of course he had. Her issues with him being here were her own problem. 'I'm saying you're not alone in dealing with this if you don't want to be. You'll both be fine because of the support network here.'

She needed to get over feeling disappointed that Ben hadn't followed her after all. He'd decided his daughter could benefit from the service Misty had told him about.

That was a good thing.

She'd make a real effort to help Tammy settle because that was her passion. Helping women discover their own resources. Not because Ben was here. She needed to accept that as soon as possible before she said or did something rash.

He leaned towards her. Caught her gaze in his and said softly, 'I do feel good about being here.'

Darn it. Now his crooked smile tried to blow all her good sense out of the water. The connection burst into life and tugged at her again. Just after she'd contained it.

She felt as if the air on the veranda had suddenly been sucked away to leave her gasping.

He looked better.

Sat back. Let out a long breath as if to unload a burden. 'I see they rent canoes on the lake,' he mused after a short while. 'Any chance you'll come for a paddle with me tomorrow afternoon and show me the sights?'

After that response she'd just had to him? No chance. None. She shook her head. 'You should ask Tammy?'

'I did.' He grinned at Misty like a mischievous boy and she found herself returning the smile. 'She told me she was too fat and to take a jump.'

Ben's glance settled on her warmly, teasingly, the way handsome men seemed to learn from birth and Ben had it mastered. 'Come with me,' he said. 'It'll be fun.'

It really wasn't fair, this effect he had on her. It brought back all the weaknesses she'd tried to deny at the beach. And later. This was not a good idea. She shook her head again.

'Chicken,' he teased, eyes dancing.

She raised her brows. 'What does that stand for?

'Can't Hop In Can't Kinda ENntice you?'

'Clever Dick.'

'What mischief could we get up to in a canoe?'

A picture of herself in Ben's arms as they drifted past

the tree-lined banks left her in no doubt that mischief could be had. But canoes had social distancing. Misty fought valiantly and unsuccessfully not to blush. She stood up and went to the rail to at least hide the evidence.

Problem was she wanted to go. A little too much. 'We'll see. It depends on what time I get off work.'

'And on the weather, and that all the boats aren't rented out, and that neither of us breaks a leg.' Ben came to stand beside her. 'Are you nervous of me, Misty?'

Misty turned to face him and she searched his strong features for the understanding he'd surprised her with before. 'No, Ben. Of me,' she said very quietly.

He smiled at her. There it was. Understanding.

'Well, you should be nervous of me, too. I'm not always a gentleman.'

CHAPTER 14

Ben

The next afternoon the sun shone warmly through the few scattered clouds in an otherwise blue Queensland sky and the lake looked extremely inviting to Ben as he walked beside Misty down to the boatshed.

Not just the lake looked inviting.

'This is the first time I've been down to the lake in the afternoon,' Misty mused.

'The babies understand you need to play sometimes. And the shed does have plenty of boats.' Ben grinned down at the woman walking beside him and congratulated himself on a great idea. 'It's not raining and neither of us have broken a leg.'

'Meaning?'

Funny how he remembered every word between them and she didn't. Misty looked up at him and he resisted the urge to drop a kiss on her lips. She really should be more wary of him than of herself. She had disgustingly strong willpower.

'Meaning divine intervention is not going to stop you from being alone in my company.'

Misty glanced around at the little boats dotted over the lake. 'I don't think being alone will be a problem, Ben,' she said dryly.

He deliberately misunderstood her. 'Good.'

She raised her eyebrows at his cheeky comment. 'Just don't try to save any birds and hit your head.'

'Ouch.' So she had a mean streak as well. He liked that.

Ben started to whistle an Irish courting tune that had come from nowhere into his head and he looked down at the copper-headed woman beside him and smiled at the world. A voice hailed them from the boatshed and old Clem, whom Ben had met last night when he'd arranged the hire, came out, wiping varnish from his hands on a rag.

Clem grinned at Misty. 'Howdy, Miss Buchanan.'

'Hello, Clem. How's the granddaughter?'

The old man's face creased into a road map of pride. 'Pretty as a picture and just as sweet.'

'I saw them at home yesterday and Ellie's a great little mother.'

'Take's after my sainted wife,' Clem replied, and Misty looked at Ben.

'Clem's daughter, Ellie, had her first baby last week. I visit her on the early discharge programme we have.'

Clem nodded. 'It was a real boost to this place when

Miss Buchanan's brother moved here, then his wife and now his sister. Now look what we got. My girl didn't have to go to a place where she didn't know anyone to have the babe.'

He shook his grizzled head and Ben began to see that what he had considered a quaint service could, in fact, be something to be very proud of. He reminded himself to talk to Andy when he had a chance, to find out how it had all begun.

'Come for the boats, have you, Doc?' Clem pointed with the rag at two canoes tied up at the end of the jetty. 'Just leave 'em there when you're finished and I'll put 'em away,' he said. 'Enjoy.'

'Thank you.' Ben reached forward and shook the old man's gnarled hand.

Five minutes later they drew away from the jetty and, of course, the superior edge from his prestigious boarding-school training proved no match for Misty's obvious aquatic skills. 'So you can swim, surf, and canoe with consummate ease?'

'Another blow for male domination,' she teased him back, and he had to laugh at his own wounded pride as she paddled away from him.

He dug his paddle in and chased. There was no doubt she was good for his arrogant soul.

'Andy and I grew up on the water at Bundeena,' she called over her shoulder.

He finally caught up and they both stopped paddling and just drifted over the clear water. She turned to face him and the little spots of colour and the excitement in her eyes made her look even more beautiful.

'Where is this Bundeena?' he asked.

'Just south of Sydney. It's an inlet on the south side of Port Hacking. Surrounded by national park. Lots of outdoor stuff happens there, hence my skills.'

'Sounds magical.'

Misty laughed. 'I had great friends. We all used to think it was a hole. No nightclubs or pubs or cool shops —just a shop for the oldies and good, clean fun for the kids.'

A shadow fell over her bright expression. 'When Mum died we had to move out to the west of Sydney and Andy commuted to med school. Eventually I finished school and did my nursing degree. That's where I met Montana and Mia.'

'Your midwife mates?'

'My best mates.' She glanced around at the lake and the other craft in the distance. 'I feel more at home than I thought I would here. Because of the water. Andy loves that too.'

I like it here because of you, Ben thought, but he didn't say it. He wasn't sure that he wanted to put that much pressure on himself. He had the feeling she wasn't ready to hear it either.

'What happened to your dad?' he asked instead.

'He died when I was about five. I don't remember much about him except he used to laugh a lot. A big, hearty man's laugh although that may be just because I was so little.' She looked at him. 'But enough about me. Tell me something about your life, Ben Moore. What makes you tick?'

Ben wasn't sure that he did tick. He'd been dead for years until this little spitfire revived him. She tilted her face at him and dared with her eyes, to open up to, but he couldn't do it. Couldn't do it. Wouldn't ruin this perfect day with his dark demons.

Keeping it light, he said 'I thrive on competition.' The willow trees along the bank looked far enough away to give him a chance, betting on his long-distance strength. 'Race you to the shore.'

'If I win, you tell me something else,' Miss I-will-not-be-diverted said. 'Something more personal than this general male need-to-win.'

Ben nodded. But he'd win.

Of course he didn't.

He led for most of the way but at the end her lighter kayak wiggled its stern at him as she paddled past ten metres from the shore. She dug her paddle into the water to skid to a stop in the shallows, facing him, and Ben threw up his hands in disgust.

He had to laugh. 'That will not happen again. I'll be out here every afternoon, practicing, because it's very bad for my morale to lose to a mere woman.'

'Poor Ben,' she teased, and stepped lightly out of her boat and onto the bank. When he tried it wasn't as easy as it looked. 'Drag your boat up here and this mere woman will pat your back.'

He followed her up the bank, considering payback for her teasing and there, under the trees, suddenly they were in a different place. The hillside angled away from them, rock strewn and scrubby, but under the trees the lake lapped the shore and it was cool and dimly lit and delight-fully secluded. A sensible place for kissing.

Misty stopped as if she'd just realised their isolation.

Ben planted his feet and smiled. 'Now, this is nice,' he said.

Misty brushed her hair from her face with her finger and faced him. He saw her notice the backpack and she changed the subject with a raised brow. 'I meant to ask earlier. What did you bring in your bag?'

So, she'd sensed how much she drove him crazy. Changed the subject. Sensible girl. He'd called her that before, he remembered, and decided that the description fit. And that he liked sensible girls.

He damped down the urges that clamoured for attention and lifted the bag from his shoulder. For the moment this was good. Since he'd almost died, he had tried to savour moments. Peace seemed to steal into his bones, dissolving some of the pain and guilt he'd held buried for so long.

Misty looked more comfortable with him and there was no rush to alter the mood because he could just turn his face and look out over Lyrebird Lake and thank his lucky stars he'd come here.

For the moment, and for today, that was enough. Good moments.

His sensible girl tapped her foot against the abandoned bag and raised those beautiful eyebrows at him.

'Aha. Curiosity.' He bent down and unzipped it and looked inside. 'Actually, it's pretty boring.' Then he looked up at her, his eyes dancing. 'I'd like one of those Mary Poppins travel bags that everything comes out of. You know chairs, table, lampshade…'

She blinked in surprise at his off-the-cuff comment and he supposed it must be a bit strange for a bloke to wish for the world's most famous nanny's infamous accessory.

He guessed it was a little embarrassing. 'Tammy loved

the DVD. I've watched it a hundred times with her. I used to do the Dick Van Dyke impersonations, and she'd laugh and laugh.'

He looked away. Actually, they had been some of the many good times he could remember.

CHAPTER 15

Misty

Misty didn't doubt he cursed himself for giving away even that much so she didn't comment on his regrets. But it was nice to get at least a tiny glimpse of what he'd been like as a father. 'Maybe you could try and remember some skits for when she's in labour.'

'Hmm. That would go down well,' Ben said. They smiled at each other. Humour in the birth unit was rarely appreciated by the woman in labour, and they both knew it. 'She's sixteen. Apparently, I'm not going anywhere near her until after the baby is born.'

'She told you that?'

'Yeah. But that's fine. I'll be a mess anyway and probably wouldn't be any help to her.'

'Poor midwife, having you in the background.'

'Poor you.' He said with that wicked smile in his eyes. Seriously, the guy looked in good humour today. A side of him she'd not seen before which she enjoyed rather too much.

'Yeah. Poor me.'

They smiled at each other again and the mood shifted, flirted, fluttering movement between them like the butterflies in her belly.

Without taking his eyes off her, Ben reached into the bag and pulled out a neatly folded rug. He knelt down and unfolded it over the scratchy grass. Glanced down and smoothed his side with his big hand. Strong and capable. Smoothing the rug. She couldn't help imagining, wishing…

'Would you like to sit down?' he said, and Misty felt that flutter in her stomach respond to the invitation in his voice and eyes. Automatically she straightened her own side of the mat until it lay between them like a tartan square of no-man's-land that she wasn't sure she was game to invade.

Ben just raised his brows as if amused at her hesitation and stretched himself out. He pulled the bag across and produced a bottle. 'If you sit next to me I'll give you a mango juice. I know you like it.'

Misty had to smile. So, he'd remembered that from the beach, had he? 'I didn't drink it last time.'

'And very sensible you were, but it's hotter today and you must be parched from beating me in a canoe race.'

'You shouldn't be the one to sound smug.'

'Smug?' She watched him mull over the word and then nod his head. 'Yep.' He nodded again with conviction. 'As the only person here with cold juice to offer, I am feeling smug.'

'As the outright winner, I, too, am smug. Therefore, I will accept your offer of a cold drink. Thank you.'

She eased onto the mat next to him and took the bottle. The brush of his fingers made her pulse rate increase and she looked away. This was not a good idea. When she opened the lid of the bottle, the cracking sound of the broken seal seemed to echo around her.

Why did her senses become so much more receptive when she was near Ben?

They both gazed out onto the lake through the low branches of the overhanging trees. The sun glinted off the serene surface of the water, the juice was icy cold and fruity, and the company was...

She took another sip and when she turned back to face him he was watching her mouth. 'You've got your own. Don't look at mine.'

He looked down at the juice in his hand as if he'd forgotten it was there. 'Wasn't looking at the juice,' he murmured. He cracked the lid and looked down at it. 'Noisy little blighters,' he said with a slight smile, and then he seemed to finally relax.

She wondered if he could feel those tiny eddies of breeze that tickled her skin, or maybe his skin wasn't a mass of raw nerve endings like hers, and he was oblivious.

The silence stretched until Misty could no longer bear it. She had to say something. Anything. 'I was surprised to see you moved into the residence. I thought you and Tammy might move into the big guesthouse down town.'

Ben looked across the water at the tall white building to the left. 'I was going to, but Andy suggested Louisa and

Ned might be better company for Tammy when I was called out at short notice. Plus, it might only be a month. B&B is easy.'

'Louisa is a champion.' Misty loved living in the residence.

'Plus…' He looked back at her and smiled. 'He did mention his sister was a midwife and stayed there, too.'

So Ben had known Misty would be under the same roof before he'd arrived. It would have been nice to have had that advantage. Never mind. She'd managed very well considering the lack of warning.

A rustle from the bushes behind them made them both turn and from the thicker foliage came the identical sound of the juice-bottle lid opening. Then the noise came again twice more in quick succession.

Ben blinked and Misty smiled in sudden comprehension. Montana had told her about this. 'Lyrebird,' Misty breathed almost inaudibly.

A small brown bird poked his head out of the bush and stared beadily at them.

When they didn't move he stepped out fastidiously as if to avoid soiling his feet and lifted the heavy tail that he dragged behind him. Fan shaped and grey-brown, his tail shimmied at them in a ruffle of feathers as he turned full circle, balancing the extra weight with some effort. The bird gave two more renditions of the juice-opening noise and then dropped his tail and disappeared back into the bush as if he'd done his job and was now off duty.

Ben let go of his breath. His mouth an open O of delight and honest appreciation.

He turned to look at Misty and she smiled back at him, her own pleasure tingling her skin. 'Wow.' Her awkwardness with Ben was forgotten in the delight of seeing the lyrebird, of sharing with him such an awesome spectacle.

'That was special,' Ben said. He looked at her and suddenly it was not awkward at all. 'You, my little rescuer are special too.' He leaned across and took Misty's hand in his and pulled her across no-man's land until he could put his arm around her.

'Mmm-hmm,' Misty said, magically releasing muscles she'd held so tight, as she leaned against him and closed her eyes to replay the sight in her mind. She'd never seen something so unexpectedly marvellous.

When she mentally returned to Ben, his now familiar features seemed more peaceful than she'd ever seen them. For these few minutes she could breathe gently beside him, relaxed and enjoying the serenity around them and this new ease brought by the dance.

THE NEXT EVENING when Tammy joined them on the veranda, Misty moved over to encourage the young woman to sit next to her.

'We get the swing, Tammy. Men not allowed. Are you a swinger or a sitter?'

Tammy plonked down next to Misty and stared at the ground. 'Swinging makes me sick when I'm pregnant.'

'I'm not a fan of the vigorous rock.' She glanced at Ben. 'If you sit here with a man he has to make it swing. It's in their make-up.'

'Dad, I mean, Ben,' she corrected herself, 'used to take me to the park when I was a kid. I loved swings then. But that stopped when he left Mum.'

'You did like the swings then. I had fun at the park

with you,' Ben said quietly. 'It was peaceful and those times are some of my most treasured memories.'

Tammy smiled and said dryly in a voice beyond her years, 'Nobody was yelling at the park. Mum loved a good yell.'

Ben shrugged apologetically. 'Your mum and I weren't terrific together. I thought I was making her even more unhappy.'

'She really wasn't terrific with anyone, but she got worse when you left.' Tammy glanced at Misty. 'He left my mum the day after I turned twelve. Mum died three months later.' The flatness of her tone spoke volumes. 'You shouldn't have left me with her.'

'I asked you to come and you said you wanted to stay with your grandmother.'

'You didn't really want me. Nan told me that.'

'Did she?' Ben said flatly, and his lack of emotion made Misty think the grandmother had lied. That he knew it but had been unable to rectify the falsehood. Hadn't wanted to cause harm between granddaughter and grandmother because both had been hurting badly.

She didn't know where to look or how to help. She couldn't resort to platitudes; these people had huge issues beyond simple solutions. She wondered if she should get up and leave but Ben must have sensed her intention.

He lifted his hand in her direction. 'Stay, Misty. Please. If you weren't here we probably wouldn't be talking about something we should have talked about years ago.'

Accepting his point, Misty nodded, although she felt far from comfortable.

Ben edged forward in his seat to catch his daughter's eye. 'You know why I left your mum, Tammy.'

Tammy refused to look at him. 'Because you wanted to do your own thing and I wasn't important enough to stay.'

Ben shook his head. 'Because I could see what the fighting was doing to you. To all of us.'

Now she looked at him but it was more of a glare. 'She put me in a boarding school. How was that better?'

'Your mother said you loved the school and I was working such long hours.' Ben sighed and raked a hand through his hair. 'But we had some good times on your leave weekends.'

'We did...until Mum died.'

'I'm sorry, Tammy. I know it's been hard for you but we've got a chance to spend some time together here. Now.' He stared at his daughter's face. 'Let's do that.'

'Okay,' Tammy said, but even Misty could hear the lack of belief in the word and she hoped Ben meant what he said because Tammy certainly needed the attention. Poor kid had been through too much, and at such a transformative age. She truly hoped that Ben could rebuild their relationship. For both their sakes.

THE NEXT NIGHT Ben and Tammy went out for dinner. His daughter might have been in a better mood if she hadn't been asked as second choice. Misty had declined Ben's invitation and unfortunately Tammy had overheard, and the evening wasn't the success Ben had hoped for.

He didn't get it and Misty resolved to hand out a few hints when she had him to herself. Things like: 'Concentrate on your daughter.' 'Don't ever make her feel as though she's an afterthought.' 'Let her know she is special to you.' She hoped he'd listen.

. . .

THE NEXT MORNING Tammy waylaid Misty in the hallway to hand out a few hints of her own. 'Can I talk to you for a minute?' She avoided Misty's eyes as she indicated with her hand the doorway into her room.

Misty allowed herself to be ushered into Tammy's bedroom and glanced around for somewhere to perch.

There really wasn't a surface, including the carpet, not littered with clothes which made it difficult to decide where to sit. How on earth could she create such a mess in so few days?

Tammy solved the problem by sweeping the only bundle of neatly folded clothes from the desk chair onto the floor.

Misty blinked and couldn't help herself. 'I'll bet you didn't fold those,' she said dryly.

Tammy looked down at the pile tipped on its side in confusion and shrugged. 'Why would I?'

'Because Louisa, who is the most delightful and caring person you will probably ever meet, isn't your slave. She's also four times your age and deserves a little respect for the help she's kindly giving. But,' She looked at Tammy and smiled. 'I'm not your mother or your father so go ahead. You wanted to say something to me?'

Tammy's gaze travelled over the mess in the room and frowned. 'I didn't think. Louisa has been super-sweet.' Her shoulders slumped. 'I've been feeling sorry for myself. I didn't even know if I wanted to come here. It's all...'

'It's a lot, I know,' Misty said gently.

'You know, you're right. Louisa is a sweetie.' She

looked at Misty and sighed. 'I've been feeling sorry for myself, which only makes me worse.'

She kicked the nearest article of clothing. 'I couldn't do this at boarding school but my grandmother didn't expect me to do anything in her house.' Tammy picked up the clothes she'd just knocked over and put them back on the desk. 'I'll fix it. I do like Louisa.'

'Wow.' Misty was seriously surprised and impressed. She looked at the young girl in front of her and smiled. 'It's pretty brave to admit that. If you want to do it now, I'll help you and we'll have it done in no time. Then we can have breakfast together.'

Tammy looked up as if assessing if Misty meant it. 'If you want.'

They sorted the room quickly and Tammy even giggled at Misty's amazement when she saw Tammy's tiny underwear. 'So you actually wear G-strings and find them comfortable?'

'Ye-aah.' But her tone said, Of course! 'I've even got G-string maternity napkins for after the baby's born. I read about them in a magazine.'

'You learn something every day.' Misty suddenly she saw how lonely Tammy was and wondered if she had connected with the grandmother who said she wanted her. Her heart ached because she could remember being young and motherless. 'You said you wanted to talk about something?'

Tammy looked away. 'I wondered if you thought my dad was okay. He seems to like you.'

Misty could hear the subtle jealousy that Tammy tried to hide and she didn't blame her. She'd only just got her father back and here he was paying attention to someone else, just when she'd thought she would have him all to herself.

Misty spoke carefully. 'What's not to like? Did your dad tell you how we met?'

Tammy nodded. 'You saved him when he nearly drowned. I can't imagine my dad needing anyone like that, but I guess he would have died if you hadn't been there.'

Feeling a little sick, Misty pushed away the images that rose. She needed to concentrate on Tammy, on her understanding how close it had been. It might help her appreciate Ben a little more. 'I don't like thinking about that day but, yes, there was a big chance he could have drowned. Face down in the water, unconscious.'

Tammy's mouth fell open, then closed again, her eyes wide with shock as if the reality of it had only just occurred to her. 'I would have been an orphan.'

Not poor dad. How like a teenager. Misty smiled. 'I'm glad you're not.'

'So am I.' Tammy finally managed a smile, a genuine, slightly cheeky, smile. 'He's not perfect but, you know, neither am I.'

Misty picked up the last article of clothing off the floor. 'None of us are,' she said dryly. 'You know your dad wants to spend more time with you and get to know you again. He's just got to learn how.'

Tammy paused as she closed a drawer. 'Does he? Or does he want to get to know you more?'

Misty stared at the back of Tammy's head. 'Maybe he wants to know both of us. But you'll always be special to him because you're his daughter.'

Tammy turned to face her. 'But I'm not really, am I? And if I wasn't pregnant, I'd still be at school.'

Misty finally felt she could understand Tammy's unhappiness. 'You can't wipe twelve years of parenting out with a blood test.' She repeated Ben's words without betraying the confidence.

'You think so?' Disbelief from Tammy.

'Of course you're his daughter. I think he's secretly glad to have you to himself after a long wait.' She looked around and realised they'd finished tidying up. 'Come on. Let's have something to eat before I have to go to work.'

THE BREAKFAST ROOM was empty except for them. Ben had left an hour ago and Louisa was missing in action.

'What have you planned for today?' Misty poured her juice.

The young woman had pushed her sweater sleeves up her arms and already she was fiddling with the neckline because of the heat. 'Nothing.' She grimaced. 'I hate this heat.'

Misty didn't comment on that... Yet. 'Well, so far I have no one in labour and we have a working bee happening at the unit today.'

'So?' Tammy raised one shoulder.

Misty went on, 'Some of the women from the community are coming and I've asked Emma to come in today to help me. Your dad mentioned Emma, didn't he? She's nineteen and her baby is two years old now.'

Misty waited but Tammy still didn't say anything. She readjusted the heavy sweater around her neck. Ran her finger under the collar. Looked away.

'We're opening a day room in maternity, somewhere the women can sit, if they want to, and chat. It's a great opportunity for you and Emma to get to know each other better. Why don't you come and help?'

'What can I do to help? I'm pregnant.'

Misty glanced at Tammy's big belly. 'I can see that. It gets boring towards the end, doesn't it?'

Tammy pulled a face. 'You bet.'

'Well, because you're pregnant, you could give us ideas about what's comfortable and what's not. Your input into what you think would make pregnant ladies feel better would be great. And you could meet Emma's daughter, Grace, who's a real delight. Get used to handling little children.'

Finally a glimmer of interest showed behind Tammy's fixed expression. Misty had hoped she was getting through to her just minutes ago, when they'd co-operated in cleaning up the mess, but then she'd turned sullen and disinterested. She guessed this rollercoaster of emotions would continue. They'd all have to ride it out.

'Plus, the birth centre is where you'll have your baby and it's always good to get to know the place, rather than turning up for the first time when you're in labour.'

Tammy looked narrowly at Misty through intense blue eyes. 'Why are you being so kind to me?'

Misty looked up from buttering her toast. 'Can't I be? I thought I was asking you to be kind to me.' She took a bite of her toast and shrugged as if she didn't care one way or the other.

Tammy mulled it over and finally an ironic smile appeared. 'If you really think I could help?'

'I do. That's excellent.' Misty brushed crumbs from her

fingers, all ready for business. 'You're the perfect person for the job... On one condition.'

Tammy's eyes narrowed. 'What?' Distrust was back in full force in her voice.

Misty shrugged apologetically. 'You have to take that jumper off. Honestly, you make me perspire just looking at you.'

To Misty's relief Tammy laughed, her hand coming up to her mouth as if she'd surprised herself. 'Okay! Gladly. I'm so over being hot.'

Tammy pulled the sweater over her head then and there and she and Misty both giggled as she draped it over a chair with a huge sigh of relief.

They both contemplated Tammy's stomach. 'You have a really neat tummy, you know.'

'Yeah. I'm getting used to it.'

'Good. Appreciate it. Because it will be gone all too soon.'

AN HOUR later at the centre, Misty looked at Montana serenely drinking tea at the desk, and then at the few chairs they had. There would be more women coming. The buzz of excitement promised a productive day.

Misty gazed at the small crowd and she felt a swell of pride and pleasure. She was a part of this. 'We may as well do a clinic while we're all here. I think I'll ring Sara and Charlotte and then they can ring other clients if they want to.'

'Great idea.' Montana looked pleased too.

She turned to Montana. 'It will be so useful to have a

women's waiting area to use in early labour. A place to relax and chat and somewhere we can all sit together.'

Montana nodded. 'Maybe we could hold the antenatal education here instead of the school hall. Make it child friendly, too.'

Misty thought of Ben and grinned. 'The Women Friendly Centre.'

'The dads might feel excluded.' Montana smiled and stood up. She rubbed her back. 'I need to walk. I'll pop over to Matron and see what else she has for us. There's furniture in storage from when we cleared this room that we could use, but I don't know how comfortable it is. The orderly and one of the gardeners would be happy to help us move anything I find.'

Misty could feel the buzz of even more excitement. This was a great idea.

Twenty minutes later Matron sent over two cleaning staff to help spruce the room. They brought a water cooler from her office as well as a magazine rack.

Louisa arrived and donated two squashy beanbag seats left by a past guest of the residence, plus a huge basket of fabric and threads and patchwork magazines. Gradually there was purpose and comfort and direction in the room as the women began to plan quilts to cover lounges and use as throws.

Tammy started off keeping her distance but was soon entertaining the toddlers who had started out shyly attached to their mothers' skirts. She seemed to have a way with them that made Misty hopeful.

When Emma arrived with her daughter the two young women drew together naturally, and Misty eased her shoulders with relief to see Tammy look even more comfortable.

Women brought cushions and plants, paintings and colourful rugs to throw over vinyl hospital lounge chairs. A crate of toys arrived from the tiny old children's ward that had closed down and the hospital gardener brought two glorious tubs of petunias to put on a stand outside the window.

Suddenly it was a beautiful room, with women quietly quilting and chatting or simply relaxing, and at one point Misty looked across and Tammy had Emma's Grace tucked into her shoulder asleep. The look of wonder on Tammy's face did more to reassure Misty that all would be well than anything else could have done.

Tammy would be fine.

CHAPTER 16

Ben

*B*en leaned in the doorway as an observer. Watching Tammy and Misty together, the ease between them, the way Tammy was helping by handing sandwiches to accompany the tea she and a couple of others began to make by the potful. And the big smile that gave her extra shine, the smile he'd not seen in far too long.

The old annexe had turned into a comfy day room and Louisa, whom he hadn't noticed as he came in, looked amused when she caught his arm. She murmured, 'Imagine, teenage girls who know how to make tea in a pot and not just a bag.'

Ben laughed. On his lunch-break, he'd come to see what Misty and the women had achieved. Saw his daughter, smiling and at ease with the other pregnant women, and noticed that for the first time she had shed her heavy pullover and wore a spotted maternity blouse that made her look very young and very pretty. Or maybe that was the smile that gave her extra shine.

How had Misty achieved so much in such a short time? Ever since her mother's death he and Tammy hadn't regained their closeness. Not only did he feel he'd failed her mother but that he'd failed Tammy, too.

Now Misty was doing what he couldn't. Communicating with his daughter and bringing a smile to her face. She'd broken through Tammy's reserves. And his.

But all that would end after Tammy's baby was born and they'd have to move on. The pressure would be on because he couldn't fail his grandchild as well. What would happen then?

Ben nodded at Misty and crossed the room. Took her hand in his. 'Thank you, Misty. It's great to see Tammy out of her sweater and looking so at ease.'

Misty smiled across at his daughter. 'Tammy's been a wonderful help and has hit it off with Emma. I'm really pleased about that.'

Ben squeezed her hand once more and he saw her look down at their fingers, entwined in front of everyone in the room. She returned the pressure before she eased herself free.

'So am I,' Ben said. 'I really appreciate your help, Misty. I kept saying the wrong things. Man brain.'

Misty pulled away and he felt the distance she suddenly put between them.

'What's wrong?' He looked across at Tammy, saw the change in her face, the now frozen look his daughter wore.

'You need to take it carefully,' Misty said quietly. 'Your attention needs to be on Tammy or all the good work we've achieved this morning will just be undone by your attention to me.'

Unintentional it may have been, but it was the last thing either of them would have wanted.

CHAPTER 17

Misty

By three o'clock people started to drift away to gather children from school, but the sense of community from their achievement had happy tapping feet going out the door.

Not-so-happy Tammy had returned to the residence with Louisa and Montana's baby, Dawn, not long after Ben's visit and Misty looked around at the almost empty room and realised that Montana was missing.

She circled the unit and finally found her friend staring out the window of the bedroom. 'Hello, there. You okay?'

'Just savouring the quiet before the storm. It begins.' Montana turned to face her. 'You need to call Andy. My contractions have started. It's time.'

Misty had wondered how her she herself would feel at

this moment, because Montana's last birth had been over in less than an hour and it was her job to keep her friend safe.

But no, she felt calm and collected, thankfully.

Montana was a month early but she'd been the same with Dawn. She would be fine but Andy had better get here quick.

'I'll ring him now.' She paused and looked back at her friend. 'Do you feel well?'

'Perfect. Though worried Andy won't make it. Tell him to hurry. Safely.'

Misty had checked Montana antenatally that morning and her baby had been positioned perfectly for birth, with a wonderfully reassuring heartbeat. But still, just before she left, Misty picked up the doppler for a quick listen and the baby's heartbeat filled the room until both women smiled at each other.

'Just to hear my baby makes me feel calmer,' Montana said, then she grimaced as the next contraction arrived. 'I'll stand in the shower while the bath fills up.'

'I'll call Andy.' Misty went through the doorway and ran chest to chest into Ben, coming the other way.

'Whoa, there.' Ben put his arms up to stop her falling and held just a little too long.

'I don't have time for this, Ben.'

'Sorry.' Ben stepped back, holding up his hands as if to say, *See, I let you go.* 'I thought you might fall. Where are you off to in such a hurry?'

'The phone.' Misty looked around him towards the desk. 'Montana's started labour and we need Andy back here.'

'Andy's wife?'

'Yes. In fact, you ring Andy for me. Tell him Montana's in labour. I'll go back to her.'

'Of course,' he said.

Misty spun and ran.

She found Montana in the shower with her back against the wall, the water streaming over her stomach as she breathed through a contraction. Misty waited for her to drop her shoulders in a prolonged sigh and open her eyes.

'You can listen now. The pain's just finishing,' her friend said, and she twisted her body to face Misty so she could place the doppler again to hear the baby.

The clop, clop of Montana's baby's heartbeat was clear and true. They listened for a minute and then the next contraction started and Montana closed her eyes.

Misty stepped back to check the level of water and temperature in the big square bath. She remembered Montana telling her of Andy's horror when the bath had been donated.

He had not been thrilled when a grateful member of the town's only family of plumbers had installed it free of charge. Montana had been ecstatic.

Andy's reluctance at the thought of water births had diminished over time with the excellent results at the centre, and Montana had chosen this mode for her own birthing experience. The bath was big, a four-person spa with no jets, and the temperature was set to suit the baby as he or she entered the world.

Misty slipped from the room and turned the volume up on the slow rhythmic music Montana had chosen for the birth.

'I've no experience in a water birth.' Ben's voice came

from behind her, quiet but with an unmistakable thread of uneasiness.

'You don't have to do anything.' She smiled encouragement at him. 'Though I admire your honesty. Was that hard for you to admit?'

'Yes,' Ben muttered.

'Montana will do it all. Since they installed the bath, fifty per cent of all our births are in here. It's hands off and all about mum.'

'Oh, Lord.' Ben screwed his face up. 'I can see my learning curve is going to be huge here.'

Misty grinned at him. 'Andy's was. Keep having an open mind.'

He really was trying, Misty thought, and it took a big man to accept he had a lot to learn from people less medically qualified than he was. She was proud of him, which seemed a proprietorial thing to be when she thought about it.

Her heart thumped. Best not to think about it. And certainly not now.

Montana breathed quietly with her eyes closed and Misty drew Ben out of the room in case they disturbed her space. At least until the next observations were due.

At that moment Andy arrived at the run, breathing hard. He had no time for pleasantries. His head swivelled as he looked for his wife. 'How is she? Where is she?'

'Montana's fine. In total control and in the shower. We've run the bath.'

Andy winced. 'Oh, goody.' He began to strip off his shirt and tie. His shoes and socks went one by one as he hopped on alternate legs towards the sink to wash his hands.

Misty felt the catch of tears in her throat as she saw how concerned her big strong brother was for the most important person in his life.

Misty grinned. 'You're outgunned, big brother.'

'Don't I know it.' He looked across at Ben. 'Never fall in love or they change your world.' Without waiting for a response from Ben, Andy reached for the towel. 'Contractions?'

'Contractions started fifteen minutes ago. She'll be glad to see you. Fetal heart rate one hundred and forty.'

'I'll leave you, then.'

Ben's quiet voice made Andy pause.

He frowned. 'Stick around. Please. Don't go too far. I may have become more used to this over the last twelve months but this is my wife and child. You know how paranoid medical people are. It's nice to know you're here.'

'Of course,' Ben said. 'I'd be honoured.'

'You'll get used to water births,' Misty reassured him, and Ben nodded, although his expression said that deep inside he wouldn't. Ever. No way.

Andy opened the bathroom door and as he paused, Misty could imagine her brother's love pour across the room to wrap around his wife. Andy stripped off his belt and trousers and unselfconsciously, dressed only in his underwear, he stepped into the water so that he could support Montana against his body in the shower.

Even from across the room Misty could hear the sigh of relief from Montana as she rested back into Andy's arms.

'You okay, love?' Andy asked.

'Now I am.' Montana looked across at Misty as the

contraction eased away. 'Now's good for a listen.' And she smiled as Misty placed the doppler again and Andy, too, could hear his baby.

When they'd listened to the heartbeat and were satisfied all was well, Misty stepped away. She turned off the bath and checked the temperature again before she and Ben withdrew outside the room.

'Now what?' Ben said as he glanced at the door Misty had closed behind her.

'Now we wait for fifteen minutes until I check baby again or until she wants to get into the bath. If they need me sooner, they'll ask.'

Misty had the equipment she needed in the bathroom and at that moment there was nothing to do except wait. She glanced at Ben and a smile tilted one side of his mouth as he caught her glance.

'I'll be good,' he teased softly, and she grinned.

There was something precious about sharing that moment outside the door with Ben, despite his obvious reservations, which she hadn't expected.

They smiled at each other and the connection she tried to tell herself didn't exist glowed between them until she looked away.

Ben

*B*en leaned against the wall and studied her face. 'Can I do anything to help? Is everything ready?'

He'd seen the tray of requirements in the bathroom and watched her take the cold pack of emergency drugs out of the fridge.

'Everything is always ready. And I re-checked this morning when I came in. So we're good. All we need is a baby.' Her eyes lit up with anticipation. 'Assuming you're going to be my second and I don't need a nurse.'

'Sure.' He'd needed to get that out of the way first. 'So are you going to talk to me for the next fifteen minutes?'

She looked incredibly beautiful to him but still so painfully distant. He ached to reach out and touch her but, of course, he couldn't. Memories rushed in to remind him how she would feel if he could just get past the frustrating barriers she'd erected. His hands tingled and his brain felt fogged from just that imaginary contact. It was ridiculous what this woman did to him. He just wanted to get closer to her.

'I've talked to you every night on the veranda this week.' Her clear green eyes looked up and straight into his while her calm words added distance again. Then she picked up Montana's chart and began to fill it in.

There were so many moments he'd thought they were getting there in the last few days and then she'd back off again. Whether here at the centre or at the home they now shared. On each occasion they'd almost reach an understanding, a closeness, only for him to be mightily thwarted.

'Of course you have. We talk about Tammy and Montana and Andy—' he ticked them off on his fingers '— and Ned and Louisa, and a lot about the unit. I want to talk about us.'

At that she glanced up and he felt his heart quicken as he waited for her response.

'Are you sure there is an "us", Ben?' she asked, and that bland inquiring face that she stonewalled him with was back. 'And here?"

Not what he'd hoped for. But what did he expect in her work place? The inappropriateness of time and place for tackling this kept escaping him until too late and he was in the wrong.

'You need to spend time with your daughter,' she went on. 'Tammy needs you to focus on her.'

'I will. I intend to. But I want to spend time with you, too.' He couldn't have been wrong about the connection between them. He'd just have to wait. Explore that further at the right place or she would continue to put other people between them even if only in conversation. AS she had now.

She didn't look impressed but the words weren't coming easily. He didn't know for sure what he wanted. All he knew was that he wanted to spend a lot of his time near this woman.

'Spend time together? We live in the same house.' She scrunched her brows together and glanced at her watch.

They still had ten minutes. He'd checked.

'What are you trying to say, Ben?'

He didn't know. It was hard to look into her cool green eyes as she dared him to be specific. The failures of the past rose up and haunted him. The things he hadn't told her. His ghastly failures.

Tammy's mother, so unhappy she'd killed herself.

His patient that he'd failed so badly that she'd died.

His screwed-up relationship with the daughter he loved so much. He looked away. 'I don't know what I'm offering. More than just friends.'

'What does that entail?' she asked.

'Not marriage.' The unexpected statement rose with force. Well, at least she'd be able to tell he felt strongly about that!

His flat declaration fell to the floor between them and lay there like a splash of blood and she looked away so he couldn't read her expression.

He'd wounded her.

He needed to explain and he rushed in despite the risk

of gashing even deeper and shedding more gore. 'I'm not up for the wedding or happy family yet, it's too soon. Too...much.' He was blowing this but he couldn't stop talking. It was a measure of his desperation. 'I've done marriage and it was a disaster. I'm not husband material. You need to know where you stand from the start.'

CHAPTER 19

Misty

Misty was speechless. Where had this come from? When had she given any indication that she was looking to him for a wedding and happy family scenario?

Good grief.

What did he expect her to say?

She'd take what she could get?

Well, she wouldn't, because in the long run, if he carried too much emotional baggage to start fresh and positive with her then there was no future. No chance for anything they might have together in the future.

Because it seemed that all he wanted was a friend with benefits.

A short-term one at that, since he'd be gone from the lake and her life as soon as Tammy's baby arrived.

This was not a relationship she could even begin to contemplate with all the complexities in Ben's life.

Misty glanced at her watch. Another five minutes before she could go into the bathroom. 'I can't talk about this now, Ben. If you can't drop the subject I'll ring for the nurse and you can wait in the other room in case Andy needs you.'

He held up his hand and shut his mouth. He should have done that earlier.

Phew.

But now her brain wanted to sift through his words. More than just friends. And she thought of Ben's daughter's face, her narrowed eyes and despondency when she'd seen Ben talking to Misty.

Tammy, who needed her father now more than ever. Tammy who predicted there wouldn't be room for her in a relationship between Misty and Ben.

She'd waited all her life to feel the connection she felt with Ben and now she wasn't prepared to see where it might lead...even if that end point was 'not marriage.'

It was all so confusing and she wanted to be self-centred and hold out for the perfect relationship but maybe more than friends was a start. Not the end.

Was she being selfish wanting more then he could offer?

She knew people learnt to adapt to blended families, risked the difficulties for the joys of being with the person who made them feel whole, like Ben did to her, but was she one of those people would could take up such a nebulous offer with such a complicated man? Maybe it was just too early to know any of this.

This was the question she needed to answer for herself before she could talk to Ben. It was all too hard now.

What was he thinking to broach this subject now? The man's timing was way off!

Twelve minutes was close enough. She put the chart down and crossed the room to knock on the bathroom door.

'Good timing,' Andy said when she came in, because he'd just helped Montana into the bath. Montana paused so that Misty could listen to baby before she submerged her tummy.

After that, Andy climbed into the bath as well.

Misty glanced at Ben who had come to the door and leant against the frame. His eyebrows had nearly disappeared into his hairline at husband and wife in the tub.

He'd get used to it. Unless he left.

Montana rested her forearms on the edge of the tub while Andy rubbed her back. 'That is so wonderful,' she said.

She looked up at Misty and said in a slow other-worldly voice, careful not to jerk herself out of the natural endorphins of labour, 'Pressure. It's getting close.'

Misty sat on the foam wedges they kept beside the bath and waited.

CHAPTER 20

Ben

Ben couldn't believe how serene both women were. The only tension in the room came from him, and he tried to blend into the walls and not invade their space, but he wasn't finding it easy.

Even Andy seemed focussed on his job of circular back rubbing with his hand, as his wife began to exhale slowly.

'Okay. The head's coming through now,' Misty whispered, and Ben blinked in disbelief. There was no other sound from Montana or Misty and nobody made a move to deliver the baby.

He glanced at Andy, who had sat back and was watching as finally his wife put her arms down under the water to push the baby into her own hands.

Then it was over.

They all stared at the baby with his wide blue eyes

open under the water and then Montana rotated his face down and lifted her son slowly to the surface.

When his face broke the surface he gasped and mewled and Montana floated him backward and forward, head out of the water, so that Andy could see his legs and arms floating. Then she rested his downy cheek against her skin as she slid him along her body and up towards her breasts, where she nestled him and Andy wrapped his arms around them both.

Tears streamed down Andy's face and Ben admitted to some constriction in his own throat.

'We have our son. Jarrad,' Andy said gruffly, and Ben slipped from the room. They certainly didn't need him in there and he'd witnessed something he would never have believed he would be touched by.

But it was Misty's face that haunted him. She'd gazed with such raw sadness that his breath had jammed in his throat and he'd felt again the drowning, racking pain of his lungs on fire.

When she came out of the bathroom a few minutes later he was waiting. He held open his arms and to his huge relief she stepped into them.

Ben closed his eyes and rested his chin on her hair. Her scent shimmered around him and her body pressed firmly against his as he breathed. How could this not be right? He wanted this moment to last—just holding Misty.

This was why he'd come. Settled if only briefly in this place of lyrebirds and Misty. He didn't know how much of himself he had to offer to her or if it was enough, but he knew his life could be vastly different with Misty in it and he wanted that.

It would be forever empty without her there.

He'd rushed her and he vowed he wouldn't do that again. He would go slowly but he would win her and they would work something out. He had to believe that.

Misty sniffed and drew away. 'I'm so glad you were here to share Jarrad's birth. I'm an aunty. He's gorgeous.' She lifted her tear-stained face to his and he dropped a brief kiss on her lips because he couldn't not do it.

Misty stepped back and her next words returned him to earth with a bump. 'How do you think you'll be when it's Tammy's time?'

Oh, hell. He didn't even want to think about it, but he would have read everything he could get his hands on by then. Anything that might help.

He rolled his eyes. 'I guess I'll just have to have faith.'

Misty smiled at him through the tears still in her eyes. 'There's hope for you yet.'

'I'm glad to hear that.'

And they both knew what he was saying. Because he thought he'd blown it before and now Misty, in the aftermath of that extraordinary birth experience, had given him hope.

Misty

An hour later Montana had settled into the ward bed for a rest and Misty was completing her chart when the phone rang at the desk.

'Is Ben there?' Louisa's voice on the phone held a thread of panic that Misty had never heard before. The last time she'd spoken to her about Andy and Montana's baby there'd been happy tears.

'What's wrong, Louisa?'

'Tammy's gone.'

Misty glanced at the clock. Late for the girl to be out, in a town where she scarcely knew anyone. It would be dark in an hour. 'Gone? Where?' Misty's mind raced. 'How do you know?' Where could she go on foot?

'All her things are gone.' Louisa had more bad news. 'I checked with the taxi service. They dropped her at the bus station after lunch. I rang and they said she bought a ticket to Brisbane, but she could be anywhere. There are so many stops along the way.'

Misty closed her eyes. Had that touch of Ben's hand that Tammy had seen this morning, that appearance of intimacy, been enough for her to feel she had been betrayed? Had that driven Tammy away?

Misty felt the crush of guilt and fear heavy in her chest. 'You did well to find out that much, Louisa. Ben's on a house call out in the bush. He'll be out of phone service for at least another hour.' Too long for her to sit here doing nothing. 'I'll leave a message for when he comes back into range. Charlotte can come and finish my shift. I'll be home soon.'

WHEN MISTY ARRIVED BACK at the residence, Louisa held out the note. 'I just found this.'

'*Tell Dad not to look for me,*' she read out loud, deciphering the words with some difficulty. The writing was messy, like Tammy's room had been, and brought home to Misty how harried and upset Ben's daughter had been when she wrote the note.

Ned and Louisa both looked grave.

'The wee one would'na talk to me at dinner.' Ned's accent had broadened with his concern.

Misty hugged them both for their genuine distress about the young woman they had taken under their wing. 'Well, she talked to me this morning and was right in the thick of things at the women's morning, chatting with Emma and playing with the little ones.'

She'd seemed so happy, right up until Ben appeared

and made a beeline to Misty.

Shaking off that weight of guilt, she glanced at Louisa who wrung her hands and looked tragically expectant, as if Misty could reassure her that Tammy would be fine.

Ned looked miserable at Louisa's distress and Misty patted both their shoulders.

'Ben will be here soon and he'll know more about her possible destination. We will find her.' She looked at Louisa. 'Do you think you could make us a little hamper of food and a Thermos of coffee to take, please, Louisa?'

Louisa needed distraction as much as they'd need sustenance for a long drive. She wouldn't have gone to the bus station if she could have caught a taxi somewhere.

'Ned, can I borrow those maps of Queensland you were talking about the other night, please?'

The older couple nodded as they bustled into action, relieved to have something to do, as Misty had intended.

How would Ben see this? He'd blame himself and fear the worst, no doubt. She wished she knew what to do for the best.

For a brief second her sight sparkled and she saw Tammy's face surrounded by shells. The shells of Ben's beach house? Had Tammy gone to her father's house?

She'd never discussed her premonitions with Ben. How did she tell him that she'd had visions all her life? That she had "seen" him drowning.

Would he think she was making it up?

Louisa turned back from the big kitchen bench where she stood, packing the requested hamper. 'So you'll go with him?' she asked.

Misty nodded. She didn't know how Ben would take her

presence, but she intended to go along as a backup driver as well as company. 'I'll ring Andy to cover while we're away. Maybe you could mind Dawn if he gets called out?'

'Of course.' Louisa brightened considerably at the thought. Louisa loved her time with Montana's toddler.

After the call, Misty tossed a few things into a small duffle bag and set it by the front door next to the little picnic hamper Louisa had brought. She heard the sound of a car coming up the road and then it stopped and a door closed. Ben's face was white when he walked in and Misty silently handed him the note.

'I missed it again,' he said. 'I can't believe it. How could I do that?' He stared at the paper in his hand and Misty watched whatever had happened in the past rise and horrify him again.

'At least she called me Dad.' Ben's voice was grim. 'I'll make a few calls before I go.' He looked up. 'What about the hospital?'

'Andy will cover.' She caught his arm as he turned away. 'I'm coming with you, Ben.'

This was a different man from the one at the beach or even on the ward. This was a cold, hard stranger who held her firmly out of his affairs. 'I don't think that would help Tammy.'

'For you, Ben.' Just today he'd said he wanted to be more than friends and this was a good place to start. He could let her share his worry. If there was any hope of them forging a relationship, he needed to learn that he didn't have to be alone.

He wouldn't meet her eyes. 'Thank you, but I don't think so. I've made this mess, I've let down my daughter and all I can do is pray she hasn't done anything irrevocable.'

Haunted eyes met Misty's as she touched his hand. There was more here than she could guess if only he would let her in. All she knew was that she needed to be there for him, despite his efforts to shut her out. 'Please, Ben—'

He shook her off and turned away. 'You were the one who said I needed to spend more time with her. It looks like you were right. It's my fault she's gone and I need to find her.'

'We both want that, Ben, and stand a better chance together.'

He shook his head. 'I'm her father. Perhaps not legally, but in here.' He thumped his chest and Misty felt the depth of his pain and knew she couldn't let him go alone. Imagine if the worst happened. He'd be alone. She knew the two most prevalent risks of suicide were family history of suicide and family history of mental illness.

Tammy's mother ticked both of those boxes.

She loved him. She admitted it now because all the pussyfooting around wasn't going to help Ben when he needed it most. Right now he needed her honesty and all the love and support she could offer.

'Today you said we should think about the future,' she said. 'Tammy will always be a part of your life. You are going to have to practise letting people in, Ben. You could start now with me.'

'No.'

'I will tie myself to the front seat of your car if I have to. Make no mistake, I have a deep pool of determination and right now I'm determined to go with you. And if afterwards we go our separate ways, then so be it.'

Ben looked through Misty as if into the darkest part of his soul. 'What if I can't find her?'

'I'll be with you then, too.' Misty hesitated and cast consequences to the wind. 'Sometimes I can find people when others can't. You have to trust me not to make matters worse, Ben.'

Ben frowned. 'What do you mean?' Then shrugged as if he didn't have the time to work it out right now. 'It doesn't matter. I'm leaving in five minutes. I need to pack and make some calls.'

This was a new Ben she hadn't seen. Decisive, focussed as he should be when his daughter was missing, but coldly and clinically excluding her from his plans. She'd been afraid this could the reality of a relationship with Ben when things went wrong.

Misty straightened her shoulders. Now wasn't the time to bow out gracefully. This was the time to plumb that well of determination.

She said goodbye to Louisa and Ned and carried her bags to Ben's car. Strapped herself in.

CHAPTER 22

Misty

Five minutes later to the second Ben opened the driver's-side door and saw Misty waiting in the passenger seat. He laughed once in that horrible mirthless humour she remembered from the beach. 'What, no rope?'

Misty refused to fight with him. 'Let's focus on Tammy. Did you find anything out from the phone calls?'

Ben started the car and revved it as if to release his frustration before he sighed and let the engine idle. 'Her grandmother says she hasn't heard from her—who knows if that's true? My housekeeper at the city house will ring me if she turns up there. Tammy's switched her own mobile off but at least it's with her if she needs me.'

Which city house? Misty didn't even know if Ben was talking about Sydney or Brisbane? Or both. Thankfully the car took off smoothly as Ben regained his composure and Misty relaxed into the seat. 'So where are you going now?'

'Her mother's house. Brisbane.' His face looked grave. 'There's no one there but Tammy knows where the key is.'

Misty couldn't rid her mind of the shells. 'I think you should go to the beach house.'

Ben frowned and turned to look at her. Unconsciously he slowed the car. 'Why? Did she say something?' His voice hardened. 'When were you going to tell me?'

Misty's voice softened in comparison. 'If she'd said anything, I would have told you. But I have a feeling that's where she is.'

'There's a three-hour difference in direction.' Ben's grip on the steering wheel tightened, his profile a picture of tension. 'If you know something I don't, explain.'

She'd never told anyone except her two best friends and Andy; she was about to add a fourth. This was it. At least she wouldn't have to pretend any longer. 'I have premonitions, Ben. Visions. That's how I found you the day you nearly drowned. I didn't see you fall into the water, I was looking for you before you fell. That's why I arrived in time to save you. You'd only just fallen in.'

He glanced at her and his face closed.

She'd known it would but she had to go on. 'I can see Tammy's face surrounded by shells. The ones in your bathroom at the beach house.' There. She'd said it. He could make of it what he would. She couldn't help him any more.

Ben swore and Misty looked away from him out the window. Then he muttered, 'Great, another one.'

The comment sounded random but Misty knew better.

'Fine! The beach house.' His eyes raked his watch. She knew he was thinking about how much time would be wasted if he turned around and dropped her back at the residence. But he didn't say anything more and Misty leaned back in the seat and closed her eyes. She felt sick. The things you did for love.

It was a four-hour drive to the coast and Misty left Ben to concentrate on the road as the shadows lengthened towards evening.

Once a bush wallaby skittered in front of the car and Ben swerved suddenly, throwing Misty forward against her seat belt. His hand came up as if to protect her and connected with Misty's hand doing the same thing. Their glances met.

She glimpsed the Ben she knew from a less stressful time. 'I'm sorry, Misty. I know it's not your fault and you're trying to help. We'll talk about the other thing later,' he said softly.

Comforted by his more even tone, the knot of tension in Misty's neck eased. 'Actually, we've a way to drive and, if you can, now could be a good time to talk. There're things I want to know about you too, Ben.'

He stared straight ahead at the road in front. 'Like what?'

At least he didn't say no and her shoulders relaxed further in relief. 'Like why you brought Tammy to Lyrebird Lake.'

He blew out a big breath. Paused and then said,

'Tammy at the lake has been a huge bonus. Despite all her talk of me not being her father, we have grown up with that relationship solid between us until outside influence blew it up.' He glanced at her then back at the road. 'That's come back in the short time we've been here. Despite her grandmother's need to exclude me. I understand she blames me for the loss of her daughter.'

Misty needed to clarify matters. 'Tammy's grandmother—the one she lived with?'

'Yes. Bonnie may have misled me into marriage with the pregnancy, but Tammy was the reason I stayed.' His hands whitened on the wheel. 'She has to be safe!'

She didn't understand and maybe they needed to go back further. 'Tell me about your marriage to Bonnie.'

'There's nothing to tell. We grew up together on the same street in Brisbane, our fathers both ran their own companies and our mothers shared charities and boredom.' He closed his eyes briefly. 'Bonnie and I had been thrown together for years but we never planned to have a relationship.' He paused and glanced at Misty. 'She could hear voices and would talk about them.'

Misty drew in her breath. And she'd just told him she had visions.

Ben smiled crookedly and stared at the road in front of them. 'Yeah. I should have realised then she was a disaster waiting to happen.'

Misty felt the world tilt as his words hit home. Like she'd be a disaster as well with her visions. Oh boy. No wonder he'd said 'Great, another one,' when she'd said she knew where Tammy was.

How ironic that her gift had brought Ben to her and now it was pushing him away.

Ben ploughed on as if once started he may as well get it all out. 'It seemed she needed a fall guy for another relationship that went wrong and she'd set the seduction up for that reason. We'd been at a party, she wasn't drinking and offered me a lift home. Silly me.'

His breath whistled in the dark. 'I tried to make it work. She did need me to be stable for her. She was drowning in well-camouflaged mental illness even then. I looked after her, submerged myself in my work when I needed sanity myself, and stayed in our marriage for Tammy's sake. But I couldn't make Bonnie happy. I honestly don't think anyone could. When she died her mother made them call it unresolved postnatal depression, which dumped the guilt back onto me, as an obstetrician who should have seen that coming. Then she dropped the bombshell of Tammy's paternity.'

'Wow,' Misty murmured. A total understatement but it was all she had.

'It gets better,' he said darkly with a long sideways glance before he returned his gaze to the road. 'Then something at work happened and I lost the plot.'

The inflection on "something" told Misty this was another major reason Ben was afraid of trusting himself. She let the silence build. Already he'd shared more than she'd expected, and she could wait for the rest. She had a lot of information to digest.

The miles passed and Misty closed her eyes until she heard Ben shift in his seat.

She straightened. 'Let's stop for coffee. Louisa made a hamper. Five minutes to stretch your legs.'

'You're a mind reader.' He looked at her and smiled at the unintentional pun. 'Do you do that, too?'

Misty smiled back, declined to answer, and the weight of his scepticism on her poor sad soul eased. By the time they'd devoured Louisa's hearty sandwiches and black coffee with cream in a jar, another fragment of their rapport returned and Misty began to suspect Ben was very glad she'd come.

TEN MINUTES later they were back on the road with head-lights piercing the darkness. They'd had a normal, non-related-to-anything-previously-discussed-in-the-car conversation at the small lay-by and now they were both wide awake. A long stretch of road speared ahead.

'Do you want to know about my patient?'

'Yes,' she replied instantly. Misty tried not to let him hear her sigh of relief. 'What happened?'

She heard him breathe deeply once in the dark of the cabin and then he began. 'One of those tragedies we all dread. It should have been simple. Twin pregnancy. She'd had twins before, everything looked fine, ultrasounds perfect. Then something went wrong, we never found out what and one of the twins died unexpectedly. I performed an emergency Caesarean and we saved the second twin. The family, of course, were devastated.'

Misty was devastated. And she wasn't even there.

He stopped again and when he resumed his voice was even softer, as if he was afraid to tell the story out loud. 'I kept thinking what I could have done differently. Should I have had them more closely watched, done more blood tests, induced them earlier? I felt so useless and that I'd let them down. I started to dread that if something like that happened again, would I act differently?'

There was no doubt what she was hearing had affected him profoundly, but Misty had nothing to say that wouldn't sound like a platitude.

'When my patient returned for her postnatal visit I was distracted and guilt-ridden that I'd let this woman down. I shouldn't have been distracted at work. Bonnie had died and I was in mid-disaster with Tammy's custody, but that's no excuse.'

It might not be an excuse but it explained a lot, Misty thought, but she didn't interrupt his flow. She had a bad feeling of what was to come.

He raked his hair. 'I knew something wasn't right. She looked the same, her second twin was immaculate and growing well, and she said she was fine. The baby was sleeping but she seemed brittle. Almost frozen into a caricature of herself. I persevered a little on her mental state but she was adamant she was grieving but coping.'

'Oh, Ben.' She suspected what was coming.

He slapped the steering-wheel. 'I should have done more, should never have let her go.' His face had become even more drawn. 'I suspected she was depressed and gave her emergency numbers to call, even arranged a visit with a psychiatrist the next day, which she wasn't keen on. And then I rang her husband. Obviously I wasn't convincing enough about my concerns.'

Misty cleared her throat and swallowed. 'You thought she had postnatal depression? Did you flag postnatal psychosis?'

'Fleetingly and pushed it away.' Ben's hands tightened on the wheel. 'That afternoon she leapt from her apartment window with her baby in her arms. They both died.'

Even though she'd been prepared, had been bracing

herself for a tragic end to this story, Misty felt the cold of shock douse her skin. 'That's horrible.'

'So was the first time I saw her husband's face. And the court case,' he said wryly, as he switched on the indicator and turned onto another road. She wondered how he could still concentrate on driving. She looked at his face as the sudden light from a streetlamp illuminated it, and it was as if he was carved from stone.

The streetlight passed and his voice came out of the darkness. 'I admitted I suspected something and didn't do enough, and the family wanted to sue me for the shirt off my back.'

He gave that mirthless laugh she decided she hated.

'As if I'd care about that. They could have it all. I did care, very much, that I'd failed her. And her baby. I hadn't been able to save either of her children and now she had died in my care as well.'

He turned to Misty and rubbed his palm on his leg, as if to wipe away the despair. A truck approached and passed, and in the moment of light she could see the pain in his furrowed brow, as if it was all still beyond his comprehension that this could have happened.

Very gently Misty laid her fingers over his thigh and squeezed it in comfort. He looked surprised at first and then, as if unable to stop himself, his hand came down over hers and squeezed Misty's hand in gratitude.

He flicked a glance her way as if waiting for her, too, to condemn him. When she said nothing he continued. 'No previous mental illness. No family history. Normal mother. Postnatal depression affected her brain after the birth, which didn't allow her to cope with grief. I let her down. I've had to live with that. It's been hard.'

Even through his fingers Misty could feel the waves of despair, even after all this time, and she wondered out loud. 'How long ago did this happen?'

He took his hand out from under hers and put it back on the wheel, as if he'd had all the sympathy he deserved. 'Three years last November.' The lack of expression in his voice was sadder than anything.

This had happened after the devastation of Bonnie taking her own life and the custody battle for Tammy? It was a miracle he remained sane. She wanted to tell him to pull over so she could hug him and tell him he'd done his best.

Somebody should have. 'Who was there for you, Ben?' she asked softly.

He shook his head, as if rejecting any thought of compassion.

'And you left obstetrics after that?'

'I had no heart for it. And I didn't fancy letting anyone else down.'

'And your friends and colleagues?' Misty didn't understand. Didn't men talk to other men like women talked to each other? Like the midwives supported each other over sad events and the sometimes unexplained and devastating losses that happened despite the best care in the world. Obviously not. 'Your family? Have you talked to anyone else about this?'

'Sure,' he said, and she didn't like the undercurrent in that one word. 'I talked to my lawyer, the judge and the court.'

Not quite therapeutic. 'And?'

His tone was flat, like the judgment. 'The QC said perhaps I could have done more but it had been an unfortunate series of events out of my control. It was suggested I could do further studies in the psychiatry of obstetrics and document the findings. I left clinical obstetrics and did just that.'

Leaving a gaping hole where he should have completed the process of grief, Misty thought. He should have gone back to see the joyful side of birth again.

Ben went on. 'I settled half of my bank account on the family, despite the court ruling in my favour.' He laughed mirthlessly yet again and Misty winced. 'The amusing part is that I've made another fortune with the book I wrote on the subject. At least it might help identify other women at risk out there.'

'I'm sure it has already.'

He blew out another gust of breath. 'All future royalties are shared between Tammy...' He hesitated as his daughter's disappearance caught up with him, before completing the sentence. 'And the rest is donated to Beyond Blue.'

'That's a great thing you're doing,' Misty said, knowing the tremendous reach of that organisation dedicated to supporting sufferers of depression.

He looked across at her. 'That was all I could do.'

Now Misty understood why Ben feared depression with Tammy's pregnancy. Because not only would he lose Tammy, but she wasn't sure he would survive if anything happened to his daughter on his watch.

'When my patient died, I realised I'd failed another person. Bonnie's mother took Tammy because she hated me for not being able to save her daughter. I still don't know what I could have done differently.' He shook his head as if to rid himself of the thought. 'It doesn't matter.

I did what I could for Tammy from a distance. I grew to appreciate my isolated life. My only visitors were Tammy for occasional weekends and my editor while I worked on the book.'

Ah, Ben. She undid her seat belt and leaned across to kiss his cheek. Because she had to. Said softly, 'You were hiding, but you can't hide anymore because Tammy needs you.' And I would very much like to need you too. But she didn't say that.

He looked at her as she buckled herself in again. 'And you.' He looked back at the road and then flicked another glance at Misty. 'You're the mermaid who dragged me from the ocean and made me join the world again.'

'You give me too much credit.'

He shook his head and then said, 'Now I have to believe your "vision" that tells you Tammy is safe at the beach house. Do you realise how hard that is for me?'

'I can imagine.' Her voice dry.

'I escaped into the science of mental illness to distance myself from the things I didn't trust or identify with, and now because of you I have to go there again.'

She began to understand a little more of his knee-jerk reaction to her disclosure and to the women-centred care and non-intervention of Lyrebird Lake Maternity. This was why he fought against the concept of the birth centre where instinct and faith in the natural mechanisms of the human body were the most important things.

Because he didn't trust at all. Didn't believe in them.

In context he'd done very well to be as calm as he had. And now he drove them onwards to the place she'd said his daughter would be. Not because of something he believed in but because he believed in her.

CHAPTER 23

Misty

When they arrived, Tammy was at the beach house. Red-eyed from crying and huddled in the big squishy armchair with her arms wrapped around herself. 'Go away.'

'I can't do that,' Ben said as he crouched down beside her. 'I love you.'

Misty's heart squeezed as she stayed back in the doorway and watched.

'I don't want to come back with you,' Tammy said but she wasn't looking at him. There was a distinct lack of conviction in the small voice.

Ben looked at Misty and then back at his daughter and sighed. 'You can't have your baby by yourself. You need to have people who care about you for support. And I want to be there for you.'

'You don't mean that. You're just saying that. I know you don't need me in your life now you've found Misty.' She turned away and Misty had no doubt it was to hide her tears.

Ben was getting nowhere and she could tell he was hurting.

Misty looked at him and signalled with her eyes to give her a chance. Ben frowned. Then stood. Tammy was vulnerable and any parent knew there were problems when an extra person appeared in family dynamics. Maybe Tammy would listen to her or at least tell her what she thought of her.

'I'm getting something from my room,' he said. 'Something I'd like to show you.'

Tammy scowled as she watched her father leave and she untangled herself from the chair and stood as if she was going to follow him.

Then she turned back to Misty.

Her shoulders were hunched as she stood there with her arms folded on top of her big belly and glared at the interloper, or that was what Misty felt herself. She wasn't sure where to start. 'Your father is trying. He wants to be there for you and your baby.'

'I don't need him.' Tammy sniffed and turned away. 'I don't need anybody.'

'Do you know who you sound like? Your father.' Misty felt like smiling but was sure Tammy would take that the wrong way.

This made the girl turn back, eyes narrowed and sceptical. Still, interested nonetheless.

Misty went on. 'Everybody needs somebody. That's what I'm trying to tell your father. There can never be too many people in your life. Come back to Lyrebird Lake. You have friends and family there.'

'I don't have friends,' Tammy scoffed, and looked away.

'You have Emma and Louisa,' Misty said quietly. 'I thought Emma was going to come in with you when you have your baby?'

Tammy didn't reply but she did lift her gaze.

Misty pressed her advantage. 'Louisa and Ned are worried about you, and that's not good for them at their age.'

'I am sorry about that because they're all nice, but I'm just a blow-in they'll forget. I'm not coming back.'

'Things happen in life that we want to run away from, but that's not always the answer.' Misty moved closer so she could meet Tammy's eyes. 'Yes, your father and I have found we might have something together, and I'm not sure if that's going to go somewhere or not. But what happens with us isn't a good reason for you to lose out.'

Tammy glared at her but at least she was listening.

'Do you really want to throw away the chance to share the early months of your baby with your family and friends? That's a gift some people don't have. It will be one of the most important times in your life. The other options short-change you and your baby.'

Tammy turned her face away. 'I'd rather miss out than be in the way.'

Misty wanted to hug her but she was scared Tammy would push her away. 'Oh, Tammy. You won't be in the way. How could you be? You drew Ben and I together when we would never have seen each other again. Thanks to you, I got the chance to get to know someone who makes me feel like no one else has ever done.'

'Pleased for you.' Tammy didn't sound it.

Misty reached out and very gently touched Tammy's arm so she turned to look at her. 'Your dad is an amazing man. And he loves you very much. I'd hate to be the cause of a separation between two people who have as special a bond as you and your dad.'

Tammy still fought, but Misty could sense her swaying. She was a smart girl; she knew her arguments were thin.

When Tammy didn't speak Misty went on. 'What if you go into labour somewhere you don't know anybody? You'll be on your own except for the midwife. Not all hospitals are as peaceful as at the lake. You need to remember family is much more important than pride.'

'You're not my family,' Tammy said.

'Oh, Tammy.' Misty put her hand on Tammy's arm and squeezed it gently. 'I'd like to be.'

Tammy looked at her stone-faced. 'My father won't marry you.'

Misty's face remained serene. 'What makes you think he needs to?'

Tammy rolled her eyes. 'Anyone can see you two are besotted with each other.'

'I hope not,' Misty said, 'because we're not there yet. I don't think your father needs another relationship right now.'

Tammy's eyes narrowed. 'Did you know my mother killed herself when she was married to him?'

'Yes. I'm very sorry that happened,' Misty said softly. 'Do you think that's Ben's fault?'

'That's what my grandmother says.'

'Perhaps she had an agenda... Or perhaps she just

needed someone to blame because she hurt so badly. The important thing is do *you* blame your father?'

Misty forgot about the horrible trip, all the pain Tammy had caused her father and the selfishness of her youth, and just felt like hugging her.

Poor kid. Misty tried to imagine losing her mother, then being separated from her other parent figure. 'I understand that's what your grandmother says—but what do you say, Tammy?' she asked quietly.

To Misty's relief Tammy squared her shoulders. 'My dad wasn't the problem. Even I could see that. Of course it's not Dad's fault my mother killed herself.' She said softly, 'She killed herself.'

Misty released the breath she hadn't realised she'd been holding

'Do you think your father should spend his whole life being sorry that he couldn't save your mother?'

Tammy stood up and kicked a shoe across the room. 'Yes!'

Misty raised her eyebrows. 'Well, that was honest, at least. So, you don't believe he deserves to be happy?'

Tammy didn't say anything but her cheeks coloured. With the remnants of her display or temper or with embarrassment or with contrition? Misty couldn't tell.

Misty took a step closer and her voice was quiet. 'You're not with your grandmother now, Tammy. You're old enough to have a baby and you're old enough to make your own decision about your father's culpability. You have to decide what you're going to tell your child. Think about what you really believe.'

Tears formed in Tammy's eyes and trickled down her cheeks. 'But if he didn't make her kill herself then it's my fault. Mum had postnatal depression after having me and it never went away.'

Misty went to the door. 'Ben? Can you come in here, please?'

She risked tugging Tammy gently into her arms for a quick hug, and to her relief Tammy didn't push her away. 'Please, tell your father what you just told me. He needs to know that's how you feel.'

Ben appeared at the door and Misty let go of Tammy and gestured him in.

'Tammy,' she prompted, and looked encouragingly at Ben's daughter, urging her to share her fears.

'Mum had postnatal depression after having me and it never went away. It's my fault she died.'

Ben crossed the room and swept his daughter into his arms. 'That's not true, Tammy,' he said. 'Oh, baby. Your mother had an illness before she had you. She had depression and, like some horrid, uncured diseases and illnesses do, it killed her. It's not your fault and, you know, it's not mine either. And—' his voice firmed '—it's not going to happen to you. I love you and worry about you a lot, and deep inside I know you would never do that.'

Suddenly Tammy burrowed her face in Ben's neck and hugged him. Her whole body slumped as if she was letting go all the pent-up anger and fear and confusion. 'I do want to come back and it was so horrible at the bus station all by myself. Are you very cross with me?'

'No, baby. I love you,' Ben said.

Misty smiled at the both of them through her own tears. 'Your father hates it when the people he loves are hurting. You should have seen him when he was coming to look for you. A wild bull couldn't have stopped him.'

'Misty wanted to come too. When I said, no, she threatened to tie herself to the seat of the car.' He rolled his eyes theatrically. 'When I came out she was already in the seat.'

Tammy tried not to laugh. Looked at Misty with maybe even a touch of admiration. 'Did you tie yourself in?'

'I had the seatbelt on.' They all laughed and it cleared the air like nothing else could.

Tammy smiled through her tears. 'He's a pretty cool dad, you know.' She sniffed and wiped her eyes. 'I'll come back.'

'I'm glad,' Misty said, and she had to tilt her head to see into Tammy's face. 'How come you got to be so beautiful and tall?'

'My dad's really tall,' she said as she looked at Ben.

Misty's heart expanded with warmth. She seriously loved that Tammy made that statement. To Misty she was saying despite everything, tests and all, you are my dad.

Ben held out his arm and Misty joined the group hug for several perfect seconds before she pulled back. 'I'll leave you two alone while I ring Louisa and Ned and tell them the good news.'

'Thank you, Misty.' Ben squeezed her hand. 'Again.'

The last word was very soft.

CHAPTER 24

Misty

*L*ater, when they'd assured Tammy that everyone was staying and she could sleep peacefully at the beach house tonight, she'd gone to bed.

Misty and Ben stood on the veranda and watched the moon rising out of the distant ocean. Ben's arm was around her shoulder. 'You seem to be making a habit of saving me. You realise if you left me, I'd backslide into the morose person I was before I met you.'

Misty looked at this man who had come into her life with such impact. He was gorgeous and imperfect and she'd begun to think he needed to learn that she loved him. Unconditionally.

She'd just realised that herself.

'You don't have to do everything by yourself, Ben. If

we're going to be a part of each other's lives, you need to learn to let me into all of it... Not just the easy bits.'

He turned her towards him. 'I've never been the type of guy to tell people what's happening inside me. I'd always believed men needed to be strong and in control. You don't play by those rules.' He looked into her face. 'You still think we have a chance?'

'If you try.' She looked up at him and rested the point of her finger on his chest and poked him gently.

He laughed. 'Ow. I'm trying.'

Misty resisted the impulse to poke him again but he knew she wanted to. 'Then try harder.'

He dropped a kiss on her lips and then another, as if he couldn't settle for just that one, then he put her away from him. 'Come for a walk on the beach. I'd like to show you my special haunts.'

She recognised that buzz that ran up her arm and down into her belly. 'Are you planning on seduction?'

'That, too,' he said, and his eyes met hers with wicked warmth that left no doubt of his meaning. The blanket he picked up was a dead giveaway.

'What about Tammy?' Misty glanced into the house.

'Tammy's fine. Tucked up in bed and sleeping the dreams of the innocent, thanks to you. She was exhausted when I checked in on her, but not so much that she couldn't tell me she's glad we came to find her. And that you came with me. She's still laughing about your threat to tie yourself into the car seat.'

'I would have done it, you know. I couldn't have stayed behind, not knowing where Tammy had gone. If she was safe or...'

Misty shuddered, remembering the fear, and Ben

drew her close again. 'She's safe now. She said she really does want to have her baby at the lake. And that she likes you.'

'I like you very much.'

'Oh, yeah?' Ben crooked an eyebrow at her and gestured across at the moonlit beach in the distance. 'Come and show me how much.'

They started down the stairs, hand in hand.

'I'll miss this place. We won't be back here while I'm at the lake.'

Misty listened to the sounds of the ocean and nodded. Of course he'd miss it here. 'You should drive over on your days off.'

He raised his eyebrows suggestively. 'Will you come with me?'

'If I can. Or you and Tammy could come.' She had commitments, too, and their schedules would not always align. They'd need to work things out.

They walked through low silver dunes that rolled between the house and the beach and the sand was growing cool from the day's heat. The crashing of the waves grew louder and when they topped the last rise the moon shone a path through the swell and breaking waves all the way to the horizon.

Misty breathed in the tang of salt and dug her toes in the sand. 'It looks as though we could walk across the water to the moon it's so bright.'

Ben looked only at her. 'You make me feel like I could walk on water all the time I'm with you.'

He stopped in a breeze-free bowl of sand on top of the last sand dune and they looked out over the waves. On the headland the lighthouse blinked its beam out to sea towards the place where they'd met. Ben spread the blanket over the sand.

Misty tilted her cheek into the breeze and breathed deeply again with her eyes shut. 'Glorious,' she whispered, and she could feel the wind lift her hair and the pricking of granules of sand as they swirled around her ankles.

There was something primal about this night, with the ocean and the sky fused in silver.

When Ben rested his fingers gently on both her cheeks she opened her eyes.

'I wanted to capture the moonlight on your face.' He studied her seriously. 'You awe me. Your strength, your compassion for my daughter and myself. I'm so fortunate to have met you.'

'Destiny, do you think?'

'At the very least,' he said, and drew her towards him until their lips met and there was intent in his caress.

She lifted her hand and rested her fingers in his and followed his lead. She could no more deny him than the breath of life.

He cradled her face like a precious bowl and she saw there in his eyes, in the bright moonlight, the quiet hope that made her wish to be as daring as he was, as positive as he was that all would turn out well.

'Tell me, Ben,' she whispered, 'why do you have the power to fascinate me?'

'Because...' he said with a smile, and when he kissed her this time it was a journey home to a place they both belonged. He made the tears spring to her eyes just with the touch of his mouth on hers.

'I adore you,' he finished against her mouth. 'Amore.' The Italian word for love.

'Say it in English,' she whispered back at him.

'I love you.' His voice strong and true. And kissed her again.

There it was. His lips. Capturing her. Making her heart squeeze the way Ben's arms were enfolding her. A magical space. A magical place. With Ben.

When he eased her down into the hollow of blanket-covered sand she lay back and watched as he knelt above her and drew off his shirt. The moon silvered the expanse of his chest in planes of dark and light and his arms corded as he lifted her head and slipped the fabric, still warm from his body, under her hair.

His fingers trailed along her cheek and she turned her face into his palm and kissed him. 'I hope your daughter can't look out a window and see us.'

'She is fast asleep and even if she woke, we can't see the house from this knoll so the house can't see us,' he murmured as he undid the buttons on her shirt. He sighed as her top spread open before him to reveal her lace-covered breasts.

He said something she didn't expect. 'I've never made love in the moonlight before. But more importantly, I've never made love with you. There will be no opportunity for seeing you fully in the moonlight at the lake. Is this okay with you?'

She reached up and brushed his lips with her fingers and she hoped the answer was in her eyes.

There was no doubt he understood. 'I want to worship you tonight.'

The sand was warm when the backs of her hands uncurled with the sensations he evoked. Ben's fingers stroked each layer of clothing away and saluted each section of bared skin. His eyes were hot and intent on undressing her until she was exposed to the moon on a pile of discarded clothes he kept layering beneath her.

Misty felt strangely exultant to be naked to the breeze and the sky in the moonlight. She felt powerful, cherished and earthy, with Ben right there beside her.

Where she lay was protected from the breeze by the rim of the saucer, with the stars blazing above and the sound of the ocean just over the hill. 'It's like a secret world up here. So beautiful.'

'It is certainly beautiful,' he whispered, and knelt half-turned above her to run his hand from the hollow of her throat, between her breast and over her stomach. He paused, soaking heat into her stomach as his palm rested over it, then he bent and kissed the sensitive skin of her belly and she trembled with anticipation as he moved to lay on his side with his skin sliding along hers. She heard the crackle of foil and knew he was protecting her. Protecting them both.

They should talk about the future. 'Ben, we should talk...'

'Later...' he whispered. He kissed her and there was no more time for talk.

His thigh covered hers as his mouth slid from her lips to plunder lower, and then back up again as he worshipped her. The sweetness of tasting him, his flavour meshed with their heat, the feel of her softness moulded against his corded strength and the possessive trail of his reverent fingers over her hip.

When she touched him it felt as though she had the same power in her own hands.

She should have felt as awkward, clumsy as an inexperienced lover, but this was Ben. At this moment she could seduce and entice and please her lover with every nuance of movement she made.

Misty arched away from the cushioning sand into his body and the sensations swept away all thought of anywhere but here with Ben.

They rose together on a wave that didn't touch the sand and Ben's whisper drifted again into the night sky. 'I love you, Misty.'

AFTERWARDS THEY WANDERED hand in hand down to the ocean, kissing as they went, and once there they splashed naked in the shallows like children. The water slid across her skin like velvet leaving trails of phosphorescence and everything was perfect except for one tiny unease. Ben didn't want to talk about the future. Would this ever change? Did they even have a future? Tomorrow would be a step towards whatever would happen.

CHAPTER 25

Misty

Three weeks later Misty looked across the kitchen at Tammy and Ben laughing at some private joke that amused them. Things were going well.

Except she was not getting any sex.

They'd agreed to concentrate on Tammy until after her baby was born before they explored their own relationship. But she was having the most erotic dreams. She just hoped he was suffering too.

Secretly Misty was glad because despite their physical closeness, something she couldn't doubt, she still harboured fears that Ben could never fully share the rest of his life with anyone until he'd exorcised his demons.

Misty stifled a yawn as she glanced at the clock. She only had an hour till she needed to get to work, but she was having trouble motivating herself this morning.

Nagging nausea made her look at her toast with a sudden tide of revulsion and she stood up, almost knocking her chair over in her haste to get to the bathroom in time.

She could feel Ben's eyes on her back as she left the room but she didn't have time to stop.

'Here, let me help,' Ben said quietly as he followed her into the bathroom and lifted her ponytail away from her face. 'I seem to remember doing this for you before.'

His hand came down and cupped her forehead.

She dabbed her mouth with the cloth that suddenly appeared. 'Obviously you make me want to throw up,' she said in a poor attempt at humour.

'I remember how I made that happen last time, but would you like to enlighten me on what I did on this occasion?'

'Something I ate?' She stood up and glanced with meaning towards the door before she crossed to the sink to clean her teeth. 'Excuse me.'

'We'll talk about this tonight,' Ben said, as if he knew she needed time to think things through on her own first.

Later that morning Misty had trouble concentrating and it was not a good time for that to happen. The hospital seemed crazily busy, not just in the birth centre but Casualty and the wards. Misty missed Montana's help so much that Andy had promised to fly his plane down to Coffs Harbour at the weekend and pick up Mia, a friend and fellow midwife, and bring her back for a week.

The upside so far, she decided, was that Ben had no time to drop into the birth centre while she struggled with the suspicion that had settled in her brain.

Was she pregnant with Ben's child?

They'd taken precautions, but every midwife knew these could fail.

AT MORNING TEA she slipped unnoticed into the storeroom in Casualty and found the box containing pregnancy kits. She chewed her lip as she stared at it. When she left the storeroom she felt the package absurdly heavy against her hip as if she had a time bomb in her pocket. She tried not to think about the ramifications if she used it.

Throughout the rest of the day she tried to clear her head a little before the intended "discussion" that evening.

After she'd changed from her work clothes, she found Ben waiting outside her room so she couldn't avoid him before the evening meal.

'We need to talk. Come for a walk with me, Misty,' he said. 'Outside the house away from interruptions.' The look in his eyes struck a chord deep inside her chest.

She sighed. Yes. They did need to do this. Maybe she was ready.

She nodded and he took her hand. This ritual had grown to every evening, something she treasured, hand in hand, warmth.

They crossed the road from the house and he drew her to the path that meandered along the lake front under the trees. It was cooler as the sun moved towards the west and a slight breeze lifted the ends of her hair and blew them across her face.

'I think we need to establish a few things,' Ben began, and Misty heaved a sigh of relief. She'd never had cause to think Ben would lie and the opportunity to be honest seemed long overdue.

'Good,' she said, and turned her head to look at him as he tightened his fingers on hers.

'Shall we sit?' he suggested and drew her to one of the park benches that lined the path. When they sat his hip nudged warmly against hers and it felt good to be touching him.

She glanced around and noted that they were alone for the moment. She wondered if she could whisper the words that loomed so large in her mind. But Ben spoke first.

'It's seven weeks since I met you,' he said.

Misty drew a deep breath and the words tumbled out. 'It's three weeks since we made love.'

His finger came across and lifted her chin so that he could see her face. 'Yes, it is. Three crazily busy weeks since I first said I love you. Why—' he looked at her searchingly '—have you begun to doubt that?'

'I'm not sure.'

His eyes softened. 'Does this morning have something to do with this indecision?'

'Yes!' She looked away, at anything else but his face, and then she drew in a draft of courage and looked back at him again. 'I'm sure you can guess. I might be pregnant!'

Ben stilled and his hand froze as if even though he'd suspected it, he was shocked to hear her say it out loud.

She rushed on, 'And I don't know what I think about that, let alone what you will think about it.' When he didn't take squeeze hand or make any encouraging signs she continued, 'I've never been late before and my breasts are tender.'

Ben sat back and closed his eyes. When he opened them he smiled ruefully at Misty and she saw he was connecting her behaviour towards him with this news. 'Thus your edginess with me. This makes sense.'

'I'm glad you think so.'

'It may have been a sand dune, but I took precautions.' He grinned ruefully. 'Lots of them.'

She rolled her eyes. 'One of them didn't work.'

'Obviously.'

They sat in silence for several minutes, both looking out over the still water of the lake. Both lost in contemplation.

Quietly Ben's voice broke the afternoon stillness. 'How long have you known?'

'I don't "know" officially yet. Without expecting miracles, I wondered if you'd like to be with me when I do the test?'

His whole face softened and tears pricked her eyes as she saw how much this small thing meant to him.

How easily she could have excluded him and missed that.

'Thank you.' He looked away and then back again, and she wondered what emotion he hadn't wanted her to see. 'I appreciate the chance of inclusion,' he said.

The chance. Misty heard his words and her stomach dropped. Was he considering declining his participation?

Finally, Ben lifted her hand and dropped a kiss in her palm. 'This will take some getting used to. Imagine if we had a daughter and I'd have to go through all this pregnancy stuff again.' He shuddered. 'I don't know if I'm ready for this.'

'Not a lot of choice here, Ben. And if it makes you feel any better, neither do I. But nobody is going to force you to stay.'

He looked at Misty and smiled. 'There's no chance of me leaving. Just give me a minute. You're a bit ahead of me with time to get used to the idea.'

'Maybe there's nothing to worry about.' She said the words while knowing, deep inside, how the test would go. But it would give her more time to prepare for Ben's response, which might be something she didn't want to hear. She hoped he didn't offer to marry her, after saying he wouldn't.

Ben stood up. 'Let's go find out, then.'

CHAPTER 26

Misty

Thirty minutes later they stood together in the bathroom at the residence with the door shut.

The second pink line couldn't be denied and Misty sagged against the wall. She'd known. Now Ben did too and she couldn't escape the consequences.

'Come on,' Ben said. 'No one knows we're here. Let's go back to the lake and talk about this.'

They escaped out the side door of the house like truant children. The sun had set but it was still light enough to see. Once they reached the path again it was darker and quiet, with no other walkers, and every now and then the splash of a fish jumping in the water could be heard in the distance.

They'd walked a fair way before Ben broke the silence. 'You okay?' he asked.

'Yes.' *I'm scared*, she thought. *Scared that I'm about to lose you.* 'I think so.'

Ben drew her to another bench but once there and seated, he didn't say anything.

Misty sat with her hands folded and tried not to read anything negative into his silence as she gazed out over the lake. He'd never offered marriage, had categorically stated he didn't want to do happy families.

Now they both knew she was pregnant.

What would she really settle for?

He took her hand that had lain bereft in her lap as he decided their fate.

She could feel herself begin to bristle. He'd taken his time. It wasn't hard. He was either in or out!

'I'm sorry, Misty. For not having the instant answer when there can only be one answer.'

Misty tried not to hope too much.

He went on. 'Believe me, I've come a long way, because a month ago I wouldn't have considered any kind of relationship, let alone a long-term one. But I haven't been able to get you out of my head. I fell in love with you, Misty, long before we lay beneath the stars on the beach and made our baby.'

She heard his connection already to the concept of their child and her heart lifted a little. But she'd heard nothing that really filled her with certainty. 'I'm worried, Ben. You don't really know me or I you.'

This time his voice held no indecision. 'I know what's important.' He squeezed her hand and looked deep into her eyes. 'You are important. To me. The rest we'll find out as we go through life together. If you'll have me.'

She went to speak but he held up his hand. 'Before you

say anything, let me explain my hesitation before you construe it as reluctance. I'm not reluctant, Misty. Far from it. I'm as keen as mustard and pretty darn happy about our news.' He squeezed her hand again and looked earnestly into her face. 'This is my problem. How am I going to ask you to marry me without you thinking it's only because of the baby?'

That was it. At least he hadn't avoided it. 'It is a problem,' she said dryly.

He shook his head. 'But it's not true. Apart from the fact we spontaneously combust when we touch, I know there is a strong basis between us to work from. Surely you can see that I care for you too much to let you go, even if you weren't pregnant.'

'Excuse me? Strong basis?' She raised her brows at him. 'We're discussing a baby, not foundations for a house.' She looked at him sideways. Or did he mean the sex was good. 'Or are you saying because the sex is good we can hope to share the parenting of our child?'

He slid his hand around the back of her neck and pulled her close to kiss her eyelids and then each side of her mouth. Thoughts scattered and dissolved. When their lips finally met Misty felt the vibration down to her toes.

'The kissing is pretty awesome, too,' he said, and Misty blinked, because she heard the laughter in his voice. This was not amusing. Ben sat back with a small, tender smile on his face. 'And, of course, we'll share the parenting!'

'Why's that, Ben?'

He smiled that blinding, one-hundred-watt smile he only brought out on the rarest occasions and she blinked even in the dim light. 'I love you so much I can't imagine going back into the dark without you.' He shrugged ruefully. 'I would have liked to have you to myself for a while, but we've still got nine months.'

She could feel excitement building. Maybe it wouldn't be so hard. He'd taken this on board much better than she'd dare to hope.

Ben squeezed her hands between his. 'What about the part where I get to hold you in my arms and wake up beside you?'

Misty could feel herself being pulled in closer and not just physically. 'I didn't know I'd offered that.' The melting of all thought and resistance was happening again and this was why she'd had to keep her distance. She had no defences against him.

He leaned towards her and there was nothing she could do to stop him because she'd been thinking about kissing him, and more, for the past three weeks.

When his lips touched hers it was like the beach house all over again. Why? How could he have such power she thought fleetingly, as her brain swirled away to focus on the touch and taste of his mouth against hers. Then all thought vanished.

His arms came up and cradled her against him, right where she'd longed to be ever since she'd been with him in the sand. He pulled back for a moment so that he could see her face, and the tenderness she saw there made tears well in her eyes.

'You know that thing I said about not being a marrying man?'

'Yes...'

'It's not true. I wouldn't be able to live the happy and fulfilled life I can now see in front of me if I wasn't married to you.' He stopped. Love shining in his face. 'Please, marry me, Misty Buchanan.'

'Are you sure, Ben? Not just because of the baby?'

'If you didn't love me, there's no way you'd put up with me.'

'True.'

'So marry me. I love you more each day and I didn't think that was possible.'

'And I love you, too, but I still hope you improve with age.'

'You haven't said yes.'

She felt the joy rise in her chest and leaned across to kiss his beautiful mouth. Breathe, 'Yes, I would love to marry you, my darling Ben. And spend the rest of my life with you.'

'Good answer,' he murmured against her lips and they both lost all sense of time for a long, long while.

When he sat back, he looked around at the dying light and the dark shadows on the lake and back at her in his arms. 'At this moment my life is perfect. Let me show you something in my wallet.' He reached back and pulled it from his pocket.

'You're not going to pull out another one of those faulty condoms are you?'

He laughed. A deep rumble of pure enjoyment that filled Misty's heart. 'I did not know they were faulty, though they had been there a while.' He flipped open his wallet and dug in the back. Pulled out a small piece of cloth. 'You know the day you left me all those weeks ago, I couldn't get you out of my mind. And for some crazy, perhaps clairvoyant,' he glanced up with a teasing smile, 'reason, I put this in my wallet and brought it with me.

Despite all my protestations that marriage was off the cards.'

He held out a small gold ring with a large single ruby. 'My mother's wedding ring. Will you wear it until we choose our own?'

He'd said he'd never marry. And yet he'd felt the need to bring this. Her worry that he wasn't invested in their marriage gave its last gasp. He'd known, even when he hadn't wanted to know, that they were destined. 'I'd be honoured to wear your ring, Ben.'

He slid it onto her finger and as so many things had fitted between them, so did the ring.

'My need to see you dragged me out of my safe bubble. Do you know how hard that was? Because of you, I had to uproot myself from the beach, follow you here, and even go back to working in a hospital, which I said I'd never do again.'

'And Tammy?' Not the whole reason then, and she leaned more heavily against him.

'My darling daughter is my excuse, not the reason I'm here.'

'Despite what you said.' She was teasing now. A lightness and joy soaring like the birds that flew over the lake. Like the dance of the lyrebird.

'We could have got to know each other somewhere else,' he said, 'but it would never have been as nurturing as you have made it here. Just another facet of how much I owe you.'

His arms tightened. 'Finally, I have you in my arms and I'm not letting you go.' He kissed her.

She loved him so much. 'So you're staying here for a while?' It was so much to take in.

He kissed the finger that held the ring. 'Because you're here I could stay here forever, but I love the lake and the healing it's brought. I'm sorry I was sceptical when I first arrived.' He bumped her shoulder, her left hand now in his. 'I was pretty bad, wasn't I?'

'You were sceptical,' Misty agreed.

He grinned. 'Do you forgive me?'

'I admit you were under stress.' She tilted her head at him, considering. 'I'll think about suitable compensation.'

'I like the sound of that,' he said.

His eyes darkened and she felt the clench in her gut he could cause just by inference. She was a basket case. Especially since she hadn't meant *that* kind of compensation, but she couldn't help the secret smile that curved her lips. 'You may not like my idea.'

'Try me.'

'Okaaay,' she said slowly, drawing out the word. 'I think I'll get you to do a talk at the young mums' class on complications in pregnancy. And share the babysitting I have agreed to do for Montana and Andy's anniversary at the end of this week.'

'I think I could handle both of those,' he replied, 'if you were there.'

The promise of other compensations shimmered between them and she tried to distract herself from inviting him to do more than just kiss her here in the dark.

She felt him smile. 'We need to get our own house,' he whispered.

'I think so,' she whispered back. Not sure how she was going to last until they could truly be together. To share a bed. To wake up together every morning.

'I hope you're good at organising fast weddings.'

'You have no idea how efficient I can be when I set my mind on something.' He squeezed her hand with a gleam in his eyes.

She suspected he would move mountains. Misty hid her smile as another amusing thought crossed her mind. 'I have this vision of you surrounded by crying babies. Maybe I'm having triplets. Three daughters.'

He couldn't hide his horror. 'You saw this? You're kidding...please tell me you're kidding!'

She laughed. 'Yes. I'm kidding. No vision. Perhaps lots of ward babies at Lyrebird Lake.'

He wiped his brow with mock relief then looked down at her indiscernible pregnancy. 'I wonder if our child will be able to save the person they love, like you saved me?'

He meant be able to see visions. She searched his face in the dimness. 'Will you mind too much if they do?'

'How could I? Without your gift I wouldn't be here. Just promise you'll never leave me, especially surrounded by crying babies.'

She rested her head on his shoulder, finally able to believe that everything would turn out right. Ben did love her and they would make a wonderful life together. 'I'll never leave you, my love, and as for the babies... Well, we'll see.'

'As long as we're together,' he said, and the wonder in his voice made tears spring to her eyes.

'Despite the fact that you can be hard work, I love your crazy man-ways. How you make me feel like I'm the most special person in the world.'

'That's because you are.' He looked down at her. 'You've taken me on, you'd have to be the most special person in the world.' He grinned at a thought. 'You know I'm going to be just as horrible to your midwife when you go into labour. I'll be even more of a mess than with Tammy and Montana.'

'Impossible,' she said, and laughed up at him. 'You'll be stripping off like Andy to climb in the bath with me.'

She thought he'd laugh. But of course he surprised her.

Instead he caught her hand and pulled her to him. 'You may call them crazy man-ways but I'll do anything to help and care for you. Always. And if I am privileged to wrap my arms around you as you birth underwater,' he shook his head as if he couldn't believe he'd just said that, 'I am yours to command.'

CHAPTER 27

Misty

*B*en had been hiding very impressive organisational skills.

The wedding began a bare month later, on the beach at midday, because Ben said that's where and when his new life had begun, thanks to Misty.

The bride wore champagne silk. The groom's tie matched her gown that kissed tanned ankles and floated above her bare feet as she crossed the fine white sand that once she'd run frantically across to find him.

The trousers of Ben's suit were rolled up at the bottom as he stood with the celebrant and waited for Misty to join him on the shore. Andy stood tall beside him, and every now and then a bigger wave would almost reach their toes with white foaming fingers.

Misty lifted her eyes to that spot on the distant

horizon where the ocean meets the sky, saw the waves rolling from the distant line and breaking ahead of her and closed her eyes to thank the ocean for giving her Ben. As she walked towards him, seagulls circled and cawed, sand flicked up and brushed her skirt hem and the waves murmured to her in welcome and celebration.

Ben had changed her life, made her realise the strength and vulnerability that came from loving another person with an ocean of depth, and what immense strength came from their bond of true love.

Her Ben looked magnificent with true happiness shining from his ocean-blue eyes, such love and welcome he directed at her that she blinked tears away.

No tears. Today was for joy.

Ben was her man, her soulmate, and there would be trials and laughter, and a world of love with him because she would be his wife, his child's mother, his family and his love, his equal partner in their journey to celebrate the highs and lows of life.

LATER, on top of the cliff above that same beach, the guests milled joyfully outside the tall white lighthouse that looked east and north and south over the ocean. In the sprawling keeper's cottage, music spilled out of all the doors and windows that were flung open to let the cool sea breeze and scent of the ocean blow through on the revellers as they partied.

And later still, when the guests had departed down the mountain to the crowded beach house to sleep, leaving only Ben and Misty to stay in the white keepers cottage at the top, Misty and Ben strolled along beside the white picket fence that marched crisply around the cliff's edge and overlooked the ocean below.

Ben held firmly to his wife's hand as they gazed over the broiling sea that had brought them together. He lifted Misty's hand to his lips and dropped a gentle kiss on the inside of her wrist.

'To my wife, my life, my love,' he said, and pulled her back against him so he could rest his hands protectively over her stomach. 'Allow me to be your lighthouse, watching for storms, shielding you from rocks, and sharing the sunrise with you for the rest of our lives.' He kissed her hair and said softly. 'Thank you for saving me for us.'

CHAPTER 28

Ben

Tammy looked back at the waiting room where she'd spent the morning in early labour. Emma had stayed with her. They all had. 'Can Emma come in when I go in the bath?'

Louisa, who had also spent the morning with the girls, embroidering a small baby quilt as she waited, spoke up. 'I can mind Grace, if Emma will let me. I'd love to.'

'Emma?' Ben watched Misty smile at the girl. They all knew Emma would love to be with Tammy the whole way through. And she was a student midwife.

Emma looked at Tammy. 'As long as you think I can help you, of course I'd love to come.' She smiled at Louisa. 'Thank you.'

A superfluous Ben was left standing outside the bathroom door, as he'd known he would be. He watched

Misty pass in front of him after his daughter. 'What if she needs me?'

Misty paused. 'If she asks, we'll call you in. You'll have to wait for that, Ben.'

He stood forlornly outside the bathroom door and listened to his daughter moan. Despite all of Misty's warnings and explanations and reassurances, he could feel himself growing more and more distressed. He paced, he tried to read, he walked to the residence and back, and finally he sat outside the door with his head in his hands and tried not to listen.

Misty came out and tried to reassure him again. 'Tammy's fine between contractions. She's even laughing occasionally.'

He hadn't heard any of that. 'She's moaning.'

'She's moaning because that's the noise her body told her to make. Go for a walk Ben. Stay away for a while. I'll ring you when she's closer.'

Then she went away and left him.

BY LATE AFTERNOON Tammy's time was close. Ben had been back for an hour though it seemed like ten. When Misty came to see how Ben was faring she widened her eyes at him. 'You look a mess. You've seen hundreds of babies born. Women are designed to do this, Ben.'

He knew. He knew. But...

She put her arms around him and hugged him.

'What are you doing to her in there?' Ben shook his head as he tried to speak rationally despite all the fear that bubbled inside him.

'Good opening noises, Tammy tells me. We are encouraging her to let the sound out.'

Good grief. He hoped Misty wasn't a noisy labourer or he'd be a gibbering wreck.

MISTY STEPPED BACK and gazed at the man she loved, thought about how hard it must be to be only hearing the hard bits, with none of the windows of lightness that occurred in the calm. 'She really is fine, Ben.'

'It doesn't sound as if she's fine.'

'Tammy?' Misty called through the door.

Tammy's voice came back, softly, a little spaced with the focus of her thoughts on the baby inside her. 'Yes?'

'Tell your father you're OK, please, honey.'

'I'm fine, Dad.' Then the next contraction came and she began to moan.

'Go for another short walk, Ben. I'll phone your mobile when she's ready. I need to get back in with her.' She shook her head and kissed his cheek. 'I can't believe this. You're a mess.'

HALF AN HOUR later Ben heard the words he barely dared to hope for.

Tammy's voice. 'I want my dad!'

Misty opened the door and Ben swept past her and knelt beside the bath to hold his daughter's hand. As he gazed into the sweat-beaded face of the young girl he'd watched grow into this powerful young woman, he thanked God and Misty, the woman who had saved him in more ways than one, so he could be here for his daughter at this moment.

And then it was all over before Ben had even realised how close it was, and Tammy's baby was being lifted to the surface.

'It's a boy,' Tammy said softly and lifted her son from the water to cuddle him against her breasts. 'Hello there, little Jack.'

She looked at Misty and Emma and then at her father as if to say, *See what I've done. How amazing am I?*

'I'm going to call him Jack because I've always liked that name for a boy. Then, of course, he will be Benjamin after his grandfather.'

'Jack Benjamin is a lovely name,' Ben said, his voice hoarse with emotion, and he shook his head at the glowing woman that was his daughter. 'I'm so proud of you, Tammy.'

She looked serene and proud of herself, too, and he owed a lot of that to Misty for having the faith in his daughter he hadn't had. He looked across at his wife and blew her a kiss. He dared to hope she'd forgiven him for taking his stress out on her. Again.

'Congratulations, Grandpa.' His wife smiled and the love in her eyes promised buckets full of love and laughter and wonderful times that he'd only ever dreamed were possible.

REVIEWS HELP AUTHORS

If you enjoyed this book then please consider leaving an honest review on Amazon, Kobo, Apple or Goodreads. I really appreciate your time and thoughts, while I and other readers, do value your opinion greatly. But most of all thank you so much for reading my book. xxFi

Holly's Heart

Lacey

Maeve's Baby

Medical Romance HM&B

Delivering Love

Midwife Under Fire

Father In Secret

The Midwife's Secret

Emergency In Maternity

Dangerous Assignment

Delivering Secrets

Midwife In Need

A Very Single Midwife

The Pregnant Midwife

The Doctor's Surprise Bride

Their Special Care Baby

The Midwife's Baby

The Midwife's Little Miracle

The Midwife's New-Found Family

Pregnant Midwife Father Needed

The Surgeon's Special Gift

Midwife In A Million

Midwife And The Millionaire

Survival Guide To Dating Your Boss

Harry St Claire; Rogue

Marco's Temptation

Falling For The Sheik She Shouldn't

A Doctor, A Fling And a Wedding Ring

Two Tiny Heartbeats

Christmas With Her Ex

The Prince Who Charmed Her

Midwife's Christmas Proposal

Midwife's Mistletoe Baby

A Month To Marry The Midwife - Lighthouse Bay

Healed By The Midwife's Kiss - Lighthouse Bay

The Midwife's Secret Child - Lighthouse Bay

Second Chance In Barcelona - coming Dec 2020

FIONA McARTHUR

Lyrebird Lake

Mia

MIA

Lyrebird Lake Book 3

Excerpt:

Chapter 1

"Is this the right place, dad?'

Angus Campbell looked at the son he still couldn't believe was his and patted Simon's shoulder awkwardly. 'Yes, mate.' How *did* one learn to be a dad in one weekend?

Angus pushed the thought away, raised his hand and knocked on his own father's door. 'I just need a minute to get my head together,' he said to the closed door. A minute passed. The lack of response was unexpected.

Angus strode to the window and peered in. The house lay quiet, something he couldn't remember it ever being. When you were brought up in a country doctor's residence there was always someone coming or going. At the very least the housekeeper, Louisa, was usually there.

That would be the *Louisa* his father was going to marry.

Another idea he had to get used to. He turned the handle of the front door and sure enough it swung open. They'd never locked the front door in his time, either.

He spread his hands in a this-is-strange hand movement to Simon, then peered down the central hallway again. 'Doesn't look like anyone is home?'

His words fell away as the door to the bathroom opened and out of the cloud of billowing steam stepped a very pink – and delightfully curved in all the right places – heat-blushed woman with fiery hair. She stood only barely wrapped in a leaf green towel, putting him in mind of a red-tipped pink rose on a dew-laden morning.

Angus learned his new son was a gentleman when Simon instantly spun on his heel and faced the other way, unlike his father.

Angus really should do that to.

Instead, he met the steady green eyes assessing his arrival and unashamedly enjoy the spectacular view. 'Sorry.'

'Funny, I can't see that apology working.' Her voice floated level and delightfully throaty and she could have been covered neck-to-knee given her poise.

She held his gaze and he lost sight of the rest.

'Can I help you?' Dewey Rose had begun to look impatient.

Impressed by her composure and a little appalled at his own behaviour, Angus averted his eyes. 'I'm looking for Ned?'

'Ned?'

His eyes resettled on the delightful picture in front of him. 'Does he still live here?'

She inclined her head and he saw the moment she caught on. Something had been confirmed.

'The prodigal son.' Her gaze swept him with even more censure. 'We heard you were coming. They all left the hospital to see the new baby. Give me a minute and I'll be right out.'

She slipped into a room two doors down and shut the door of one of the bedrooms. Firmly.

Angus blinked and stepped back. Not sure if he was allowed into his own father's house or not.

'She can handle you, dad.' Amusement laced Simon's voice. 'Watch out for that one.'

Angus turned to look at this young man he barely knew, his son, and tilted his head. 'Really? On what knowledge do you base that assumption?

Simon grinned. 'On my knowledge of women.'

So that explained it? The kid wasn't even twenty.

'Yep.'

Angus shook his head in mock awe. 'How can you have such knowledge of women at your tender age?

Simon flashed him a cheeky grin and Angus felt that pang again. The pang he felt every time he remembered that he'd missed seeing this amazing young-being grow up.

'Just do.'

No doubt he himself would have been a different man if he known he had a son. Angus felt the anger rise again and he damped it down ruthlessly. It was okay. He knew about Simon now.

Simon went on. 'Because I have four sisters. Plus,

you've been working eighty hours a week all over the world since I was born so haven't had time to learn about dating.'

Angus thought of the extremely desirable women he had escorted for short periods in far-off places over the years and decided his son didn't need to know his father had more than a little experience himself.

'So, you know about me but not the other way round?'

'Mum filled me in.'

Angus swallowed the biting response he wanted to make. But his throat still tightened. That would be the woman who told Angus she miscarried this boy-man twenty years ago. The one woman he'd loved and wanted to marry who had married someone else.

His son went on. 'She said she had to tell me about you in case something happened to her.'

Angus drew a discrete breath to remove the overtones from his voice. 'Well, I wish she told me about you earlier...'

Grey eyes met grey and he saw a little of his own anger in Simon's usual good nature. 'So do I.'

Mia Storm, oblivious to the amusement she left in her wake, shut the door firmly and lent against it. Hunk alert. There was something about that big, craggy man at the door that sucked the breath from her lungs and accelerated her heart rate in a totally unwanted response. Had that been response to general hunkiness or the man?

All okay. It was okay. Just a hormonal reaction that she could control. Would control. She was coping with pregnancy hormones, wasn't she?'

She'd come to Lyrebird Lake to start anew, build a life

for her unborn child and herself, fresh and immune to the destructive hold men like Mr Hunky seemed to have over her.

Not precisely him because she didn't know him from Adam, but there was that look in his eyes that said he'd like to take half a dozen steps forward and carry her back into the bathroom and kick the door shut.

Her arms broke out on goosebumps.

And she'd wanted to be carried there.

Where the heck had that come from? Heat scorched her cheeks and she stepped away from the door as if there was a blow torch on the other side.

He was Ned's son, for crikey sake. The man who had walked out of his father's house twenty-years ago and not bothered once to see if dear, sweet Ned was still alive. Or so her friend, Misty, had said.

No doubt after he had had his way with her in the bathroom, he be gone from her life just as quickly as the man who run from the child growing inside her.

Stop!

Nobody was having their way with anybody in the bathroom and she needed to take control. She sucked in a breath. Felt the calm return. Good.

Mia ripped off the towel and pulled on her briefs. Now that she came to think about it there have been two people at the door, but she could remember anything about the other one except that he turned around, as he should, when confronted by person barely dressed in their own house.

Not like... Angus that was his name. She clipped her bra and spun it to the front to slide her arms in. The big A, more likely. Mia stepped into her green shorts and yanked her "Fight Breast Cancer" T-shirt over her head. She glanced in the mirror and her hair bounced red ringlets all over head like a frenzied mattress. She squeezed and flattened the coils to her head, until most were confined by the elastic band in the middle.

She hated the unruliness of her hair because it was another thing she couldn't control.

He'd been tall so she pushed her feet into high-heeled sandals and straightened her shirt over her slightly rounded waist. She didn't look pregnant. Yet.

Pulled her shoulders back and lifted her chin. 'Right then.'

Buy the rest. Out 30 December

Lyrebird Lake
Emma
Book 4
30 Jan
Pre-order now
New book every month
FIONA McARTHUR
Lyrebird Lake
Emma

FIONA McARTHUR

Midwife on the ORIENT EXPRESS

DEAR READER

Have you ever wanted to experience the romance and glitz of the world's most glamorous train journey the Venice Simplin Orient Express?

A few years ago I travelled in style with my writing friend, Alison Roberts, from Venice to London on the famous Wagons Lit. What a magical journey it proved.

We always had the idea that we would write about our experiences and my original book was called Christmas With Her Ex. How much I loved the writing and for a long time I've wanted to spend more time with those characters.

As you know, at heart I will always be a midwife, so I'm even more excited at the rebirth of this story years later with the chance to delve deeper into my midwife Kelsie as well as the people she meets on her adventure, to move technology

and details into the present time, and to rechristen the

whole fun ride, "MIDWIFE ON THE ORIENT EXPRESS."

From the canals of Venice to the soaring Italian Dolomites, crossing snow-covered valleys and burrowing through the mountains of the Austrian Alps, with men in tuxedos and women in sequins... It was a journey we will never forget.

You can ride with my heroine, Kelsie Summers, an independent midwife who has always dreamed she'd ride this train one day, and Lucas Larimar, the man she left outside the register office fifteen years ago.

For Lucas, offering his seat to Kelsie in Venice two days before Christmas is tough, but leaving her alone with his meddling grandmother is a hundred times worse.

Lucas can't believe the surge of emotion as he looks at the woman he crossed a world to get away from and who broke his heart.

Through the night and into the next glamorous thirty-six hours our train blazes a trail across the countryside. Whoosh past the bells and flashes of light of railway crossings while some, but not all, of its occupants sleep in their little beds until dawn outside Paris.

Join me for drama and fun as Kelsie and Lucas rediscover, and then lose each other again, while the train shoots through Europe.

What else can happen to Kelsie after the tunnel to England, the white cliffs of Dover appear, and she passes keeps and stone walls and English backyards until finally she reaches the bustle of London?

Is it a dream that didn't materialise or is it the magic of Christmas? I wish you a happy journey and a wonderful Christmas! xxFi

Excerpt

Lucas

The seagulls were screaming — or maybe it was Lucas.

Twelve-year-old Lucas Larimar saw the blue-green wave hit the rockpool wall and engulf his mother before tumbling her over and over like a doll – smashed like the broken shell he'd cast earlier into the waves – until her body fell back onto the rocks outside the pool.

Sand flew from his feet and his hands pumped at his heaving sides but it took too long to get there. His dread grew along with his gasps. He should have pleaded with her not to go back. The words had wanted to come.

He should never have held them back.

'A quick look for Daddy's ring,' she'd said. 'I must have dropped it in the rock pool.'

But he'd known the tide was coming in. They both had. The last wave had made them run from the rocks. And now...

'Look after your mother,' Dad had said as he'd left that morning. 'You be the man of the house when I'm at work.'

But Lucas hadn't looked after her. He'd stayed by the car as she'd told him.

More waves... And then another...

People were shouting, running, reaching his mother as he couldn't. They'd get her.

But no.

A man dragged her from the water and as Lucas gasped and fell down on the sand his mother lay limp like the seaweed that curled, dry, and dead, beside her face and her eyes changed as the light went out of them. Her long hair trailed the sand and he reached for her face before someone pulled him back.

Nothing would ever be the same.

Her eyes weren't seeing him... He knew.

His mother lay dying and it was all his fault.

1 KELSIE

Fifteen years later. Venice. Two days before Christmas.

Kelsie Summers floated past St Mark's Square nestled in her ornately carved and gilded gondola and thought of last night's Christmas-themed mass at St Mark's Cathedral.

When she closed her eyes the lights and sounds seemed still to float in the air, and prickling goose-bumps made her rub elbows and upper arms as she sighed happily and leaned further back in her red cushioned seat.

Strings of Christmas fairy lights over the Bridge of Sighs had winked last night, and now, though extinguished, hundreds of strings of sleeping bulbs decorated the canals and bridges of Venice like spiderwebs as she made her way to the station.

The station. She couldn't wait.

Her suitcase lay on the bottom of the gondola packed full of nativity scenes in glass, tiny gilt trees, and Murano glass Christmas ornaments for her friends.

Another crumbling mansion on the Venice waterways had sun-catching crystal mangers and cherubic angels in its lower windows and as she watched the last of them fade into the distance her strapping gondolier ducked under the final bridge. Two men, in the gondolier's black hats with red ribbon, stood with their backs to the canal, in iconic stance, and behind her a tunnel of criss-crossing bridges wove over the waterways.

The end of two weeks of magic, starting with a cruise into Venice, the trip of a lifetime and she'd done very well on her own. She'd made this long-time dream come true. And there was more to come.

The bow of the long black boat kissed the wharf and the gondolier swung Kelsie's bag up onto the narrow boardwalk the same way as he held the craft steady, with little effort and studied Venetian nonchalance.

She'd chosen the strongest-looking gondolier for just that reason. She'd hoped he'd hop out and drag her bag up to solid ground even but she feared that was not to be.

Her not very sensible shoes touched the planks of the jetty and she swayed for a minute but she'd chosen her more formal attire for a reason. In honour of the coming journey. Heels would be worth it.

She pulled her soft overnight bag higher up her shoulder and when she turned, her tassel-hatted hero waved cheerfully as he pushed off, abandoning her and her suitcase where it stood, one wheel jammed in the rickety planking crack a dozen feet from solid ground.

No gentlemanly assistance then. Right.

Kelsie carefully dislodged the caught wheel – not a good time to snap off the saving grace of mobility on her bulging monstrosity of a bag – before dragging it up the boardwalk to the concrete. Ground as solid as she could get in Venice.

Her lifelong travel dream was coming to an end. Modern-day women didn't need male help, Kelsie told herself, but the Stazione di Venezia and the Santa Lucia steps mocked her as she glanced down with a grimace and contemplated a step by step, drag and pull of her bag times twelve, while wearing high heels.

A passing Venetian 'gentleman' flicked his nicotine-stained finger at the tiny alley that ran up the side of the building for those who didn't want to hump their belongings up the mountain to the station and she smiled her thanks.

She'd arrived in Venice in a blaze of anticipation via the front entrance to the railway station and it seemed fitting, she wasn't sure why, to be slipping home to the real world of work and her solitary flat in Sydney, in the back way.

Her spirits soared again.

Once she'd dragged this bulging brick of a suitcase inside here, her train would be anything but the back way.

The last part of her journey — the expedition she'd dreamt of since her long ago boyfriend had mentioned his English grandmother embarked on it nearly every year. As a small town Australian, the idea of a train journey through the Austrian Alps all the way to Paris, then on to London, had captured her imagination.

Back then it had seemed impossible to ever make that trip. Another goal reached. Venice to London via the Orient Express — the world's most glamorous train – and she would be one of those passengers.

Hence the reason she wore her second-highest heels and her new cream Italian suit. Maybe not so romantic doing it by herself, she conceded, but still very glam. Kelsie straight- ened as she entered the cavernous world of departures through her small doorway and popped out beside a tourist shop adorned with miniature gondoliers' hats.

She searched the signs.

Platform One.

Kelsie glanced around. Remembered the inside of Saint Lucia from arrival — and yes, still it presented like any other railway station — grey concrete, cold underfoot, traveller- filled bench seats, matching-luggage families huddled together.

She'd entered at the correct platform, arrived at the specified time, so where was the blue and gold emblazoned wagon of the Orient Express?

Tucked in a corner she spotted a small white sign, ordinary, unostentatious, a few fully occupied seats positioned around it.

The sign read, 'Meeting Point for Venice Simplon Orient Express'.

2 LUCAS

Lucas Larimar watched the shoulders of the smartly dressed woman sag as she peered under her dark cap of hair with the perplexed countenance of the unseasoned traveller. Her head dipped down at what must be a horrendously heavy suitcase.

Amused, he wondered if she'd dare try and perch on top of it. He sighed and stood to offer his seat, brushing away the niggling feeling that he knew her.

He didn't. He was in Venice. And if he didn't offer her his seat Gran would poke him with her silver-topped cane as if he were a kid until he did. Unfortunately, Gran knew she was his one big weakness and the only woman he loved.

He caught his gran's glance as she nodded approvingly

and bit back a grin. Despite her age she looked like a million Euros in her pink jacket and skirt with her snow-white hair fresh from her Venetian stylist.

The pink Kimberley diamonds at her wrist and throat glittered under the electric lights. Lord, he would miss the old minx when she was gone. Had to be the reason he was standing here in the first place.

He had very special clients, the Wilsons, a couple he'd worked with for years, whose tenuous assisted pregnancy had been particularly challenging, and they were all on tenterhooks until Connie Wilson had this baby safely delivered.

He'd promised her influential husband, Harry, and more importantly the nervous Connie, he'd be available twenty- four seven. He was still a helicopter ride away if needed.

But, he should be somewhere closer to them, instead of sitting on a train for the next thirty-six hours playing nurse- maid to an eighty-year-old lady who should be at home, knitting.

Even he laughed at the idea of Gran doing anything of the sort.

The original stickler for good manners was becoming impatient and inclined her head sideways towards the woman several times and he settled her with his nod. He'd better be quick about it.

If Gran was going to order him around like a school-boy, Lucas mused, this could prove to be a very long thirty-six hours. He stepped closer to the woman and spoke from behind her. 'Excuse me, Madam. Would you like my seat?'

The woman turned, their eyes met, and recognition

slammed into him harder than an express train pushing a suitcase twice the size of hers.

Good grief. Thick-lashed eyes. Snub nose. That mouth. The mouth it had taken him, admittedly in his callow youth, two years to banish from his mind. A face that seemed outlined with a dark crayon line of accent instead of the blur every other face seemed to hold.

Fifteen years ago.

Kelsie Summers.

'Or perhaps you'd rather stand.' Luckily that was under his breath because his grandmother's eagle eye had spotted his reaction.

Stunned blue eyes stared frozenly back at his. He saw the shudder in her fragile alabaster throat as she swallowed, and then her tongue peeped out. Yes, you damn well should lick your lips in consternation, he thought savagely, since you left me at the registry office, cooling my heels.

He gestured to the seat beside his grandmother with all the reluctant invitation of a toddler giving away his last lollypop. Damn if he didn't feel like sitting down again and turning his back.

But that would be childish and he hadn't indulged in such weakness for a long, long, time.

But to meet her here... If he knew his grandmother it would be the perfect diversion from the boredom that, despite her assurances, would ultimately descend on her before they reached London.

They would meet again on the train.

There must be a Gollum filled with bad luck standing behind him. He almost turned to see...

End of excerpt.

Reviews for Midwife On The Orient Express.

… a lovely story. I was fascinated by the descriptions of the experience of riding the train, it sounds fantastic!

…a charming read. The magic of travelling on the Orient Express is something I've never experienced but would dearly love to.

…I felt like I was on this train trip with them, the descriptions were fabulous, and I loved Winsome Lucas's grandmother she is adorable, there were lots of happy smiles reading this one as Lucas and Kelsie found their wonderful HEA.

Buy here

ebook **books2read.com/u/4AzBxp**
print https://www.fionamcarthurauthor.com/bookstore

FIONA McARTHUR

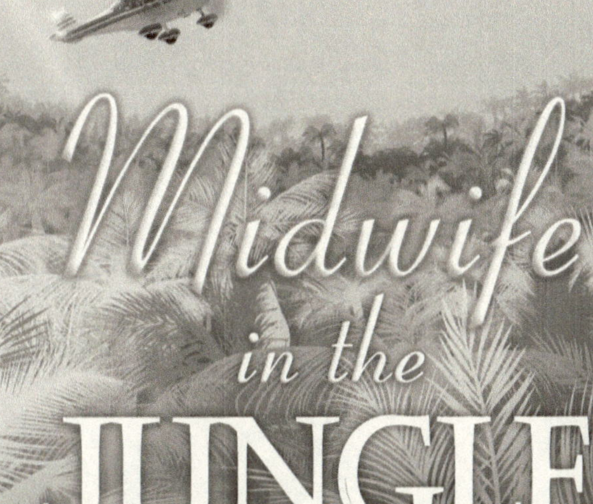

MIDWIFE IN THE JUNGLE.

Excerpt

'Jonah. Can you hear me?'

Jonah Armstrong groaned as he surfaced through the fracturing thinness of his delirium towards the distant sound. There was something about the cadence in her voice that calmed him. Something that made the ghosts fade and lose potency.

The nightmare receded as he eased out of the strangling mists and opened his eyes a sliver as he tried to focus. Even his eyelids hurt when he cracked them and the struggle with their weight felt too great. The face of the speaker hung surrounded by a halo of light, which seemed reasonable for an angel, and she must be an angel because he didn't recognise her.

And he was dead.

Jonah's tongue shifted stickily on the roof of his mouth as he tried to speak. His lips opened and closed.

The halo approached as she brought her face closer to catch his words.

'Melinda's ring.' His voice came out barely a whisper, fractured and uneven.

'There is a ring on your finger, Jonah.' Softly. Calmly. Her voice.

He sent the message to his brain to lift his eyelids again, but the synapses weren't listening. The peppermint of her breath touched his face. Did angels chew peppermint?

'Jonah, the airline ticket in your wallet says you flew in from New Guinea two days ago. Are you taking anti-malarials?'

This time his muscles obeyed, and he could discern her eyes were dark and caring. His sluggish brain finally articulated his answer. 'Last night. In pocket.'

Jacinta slid her hand into his trouser pocket, retrieved the tablets and read the label. Then she stepped back from the bed and spoke to someone. 'If it's malaria, presumably this strain is resistant to Doxycycline. We'll just have to try something else,' she murmured.

Everything went black. Time passed. The ghosts returned.

When Jonah regained consciousness, he accepted he hadn't died. Too many aches for death. Close thing. Eyes forced open, he stared at the tiny square of light coming from behind the edge of the curtain as if it were a signpost to the normal world. Tentatively he stretched his legs, and although the ache pulled and resisted in his muscles, the flooding pain of movement from yesterday had subsided.

Warily he turned his head on the damp pillow as

someone approached his bed. Still fuzzy, he squinted to bring the woman's two heads together. Once they'd fused, he could see she had the darkest brows he'd ever seen above brown eyes filled with the compassion he'd heard yesterday.

So, she wasn't an angel. Angelic, but real.

'Good morning, Dr Armstrong. I see your fever's broken.'

Jonah swallowed and licked his lips as he tried to form the words his brain had trouble framing. She must have noticed because she moved swiftly to the bedside table, picked up a plastic tumbler of water and directed the straw into his mouth before he even figured out his desperate thirst.

He sighed as the coolness slid down his throat and the roof of his mouth no longer tasted like the entrance to a bat cave.

'Thank you.' His voice cracked with weakness and he despised the sound. Still, it was better than being dead.

'Your strain of malaria was a particularly vicious one and I thought for a while we were going to lose you.'

He could tell she was genuinely glad he was awake, and the knowledge warmed the last of the cold spots in his body. Being alive was good. He'd survived tropical snakes, spiders and crocodiles in the depths of New Guinea only to succumb to a mosquito in the height of civilisation. The idea vaguely amused him.

'And you are...?' He could feel the strength seeping back into his limbs and there was sweetness to the feeling. A stark reminder that he shouldn't take his body for granted. He'd done that for far too long.

'Jacinta McCloud. I'm one of the doctors from the emergency department here at Pickford.'

She smiled and suddenly he felt light-headed again, but this time for a different reason. The old barriers refused to assemble as he'd trained them. Blame the malaria – or fate, or timing -- because there was something about this woman that slid like a stiletto straight to the core of him in a way he hadn't experienced before.

His life did not include women you couldn't leave behind!

Almost as if she sensed his panic, she turned away and walked to the window. He watched the way she moved, her back ramrod straight like Sister Angelina, the solitary missionary nun he'd grown up around in New Guinea. Yet somehow, it didn't come off. She couldn't hide the fact she was unmistakably a woman.

And there he was again, speculating about someone outside the parameters of his life, and he didn't do that. Angry with himself, he pulled his disgustingly weak body upright past the pillow until the cold backboard of the bed was hard against his spine, and he had control.

Buy link